Nos Amo

I

June 7th,

    the day of the trial:

"It was an age of disarray." Peter *said* to his host, "I was, *perhaps*, misguided."

"Then let's start over...**[tape paused and started again]**...did you attend the defendant's lecture?"

"*I did.*"

"And what do you *surmise* was the purpose of the lecture being given?"

"Excuse me?"

"Why did anyone care that *it was* being given?"

"Well, we had all realized, after a certain point, that *all* of the disciplines were coming up against *the same* problem, *that is*, they had *all* reached a limit that *was equally* un-encompassable for each discipline *as it was was* an enigma in itself..."

"...can you please get to *the point?*"

"Okay, *I am* attempting to say *what it is that happened.*"

"Yes, *we are aware*, this is your third attempt."

"Okay, *well what more do you want from me?*"

"Why was the lecture attended by over five-thousand people?"

"*Nobody knows.*"

"Nobody knows? Surely you academics have *some* explanation."

"That's what I am trying to tell you...it was just one of those things, *nobody knew what to call it*, it was more like *a frustration* than a limit."

"*Now we are getting somewhere.*"

"Okay, well what happened was *nobody could figure out how to* adjust their methodology to *not be* dependent upon a structured system of language *that was dependent upon history...*"

"*Again*, what does *that* mean?"

"Well, it's more or less like *this*, imagine you are on a boat out in the ocean..."

"...a boat?"

"...yeah a *boat,* and you are with *about* fifty other *people,* and each of you needs to adjust towards a respective task on the boat, for a number of different reasons, they'd get sick from not working or being in the sun, or be in the sun too much, or they'd get idle hands and distract from *the focus of keeping the boat intact, because the boat is always functioning, it only is paused when it has reached a destination,* but when it's traveling everyone needs to be doing something, and because it's a boat, things people do *do* have repercussions that are contained *by the boat, meaning,* if people *eat* too much food there may be *fish*-ing but a certain degree of stock needs to be kept, especially *of fresh water,* and if people fight with each other *it lasts*, as the emotions maintain themselves in such close quarters..."

"...okay I get it, I am *on a boat*."

"*Now*, imagine you had never done any of this before, and neither had anyone else really, imagine *this* was such a vast boat ride that whole families needed to be on board, whereas only people out venturing had gone short distances, so imagine what the discussions would *be* like when it came to understanding *how* it is each person *is* to take task and responsibility towards the well-being of *the boat*."

"There would be a lot of *arguing*."

"*That's right*, now imagine that over time *the arguing* subsided for whatever reason and everyone got to their respective task alright and things were moving along, but *then*, *then* there was no arrival, the destination was just never *there*, mischarted perhaps thousands of miles, and *yet* still nothing in sight for all these efforts to have reached..."

"...*sounds like*...mutiny..."

"Now imagine how people would react to such *an event, it would question the integrity of the entire structure the boat had settled into...*

beginning

"...well, that as much is obvious..."

"...but now, imagine, that as I had said *this was realized*, imagine if it wasn't, imagine if nobody *really* knew how far the destination was, but they knew it was very long, and they assumed over time that it was just still a long ways away, so families and generations started to emerge on this boat..."

"...I thought you said the boat contained all of the repercussions, how could it sustain generations?"

"My point exactly, now not into the fleshy details, but rather, let's suspect how it is these members of the boat would start to regard the purpose of their tasks, if it was they had to start to make difficult choices."

"Well, they'd either have fought into some order and sorted tasks based on that, or they'd have decided which tasks were the most important and determined who would best be able to get that role."

"Yes, I'd agree, and I'd have to say, if you think, it might take more than just fighting for them to get to settle on this, because they know they can't just kill everyone, it's a boat that needs many hands."

"So you are saying they'd have to all be arguing about God."

"Well no not my point, but quite a point indeed, and it's the kind of punctilious talking that would occur indeed, something highly specialized towards how the events of the boat would relate to the future of the boat, something that would need a transcendent point of view from which everything could be oriented, especially if this boat failed to discover a leader..."

"...a leader? I'd imagine that would have been settled very early on..."

"...Well, how do you lead a boat that has a destination that will never arrive, how could you ever convince anyone else you knew where you were all going, there would be no way to confirm."

"I see your point, continue."

"Okay, now with no leader that could last, and a destination that has not yet arrived, yet still the collective responsibility and necessity of sustaining the process of the boat, it is we arrive precisely where it is this frustration emerged within academia."

"Excuse me...*this really is how all these academics make their points, smoke and mirrors.*"

"Well, again, you are not wrong, you are quite astute **[REDACTED]**, I'd imagine you'd make an excellent academic assistant.

Yet, what it is I am attempting to explain, is that over the process of this boat coming to arrive, it is that in its arriving there arises a sense of something more, something that could be said to be a destination within *the destination,* that is, that each respective task could instead be seen as the limitation of the boat and thus rather than just maintaining the boat each task is seen as capable of being adapted towards some greater function that could potentially get the boat to determine some form of *sustainability,* over time, fishing would get better, sail use would get better, rationing, exercise, all facets could be developed and adapted, and some relationship between the people on the boat would reflect this experience."

"What do you mean by *some* relationship?"

"Well, it wouldn't be everything, because without a leader how could it be enforced, you'd have to think that after a long, long, long enough time of chaos something settled, and things started to just click, that is, each respective task *would realize* that they had such an ability at hand, and they would all seek to develop it in an effort to advance beyond the stages of difficulty that had resided within the collective experience before, not because it is for itself something to do, but because the motion of the boat settling *would be* this, and this is where it gets hard to explain, but what it means is more or less like saying this...

2

Second Class

"So who wants to review what it is we know about Professor Cinotau?"

"Well...I will."

"Thank you James, please prepare it for the next lecture so that we can figure out where this discussion can go.

You know, it's interesting Professor Cinotau was brought into the narrative in this way...I had been at home the other day and I was leafing through an old notebook I had, one of those precious letter-bounds from my younger days, when I would steal into the library under the benediction of some sacred thought, or at least one I was holding holy *enough* to sway the boredom of my lessons and instil into my learning some inspiration, so that under these auspices I could discover upon some book of relief onto which my seeking fingers would land without cause other than so it had there been, and then within the pages I would leaf towards where the rhythm of whatever tune had been playing through my mind found a bend and there I would descend into the words, looking at them as if they were to explain *it all*, what were the perjugations of my boredom, what held me in such chalid exile, what could *the world* show to me now if such the world as it mightily *could* be *would* show itself to me right in that moment, and there those words would have my most sincere attention, for in my cold indifference still embered a spark of hope for something *beyond all of this*, and with this right movement I had given it the flourish of its own incandescent being so that its long trail of combustion could reach from the seat of my soul and enliven within my gaze the harmonic notes of a greater thread of sound, one deep within the words that *knew* what they meant, that gave common and collective purpose to their becoming so that they *all made sense* and they all made sense to me right now, *right then*, in that moment my unknowing, young minds had sought beyond themselves, to leave their embers within stone, so that one day, arisen, again they could spark a flame, *here*, I have the notebook right in my desk," Professor Dillinger reached down to collect the notebook from the withdrawn desk drawer.

He held it up for a moment, unopened, and inspected it, he didn't reveal to the students any emotions, but held the thought a moment longer, and then spoke, "What I am going to read to you is going to come out of context, but I want you to know, each moment has the potential for each thing within it to *become* the context, *through us*, so even though we may not yet be able to see it, *there is* a way by which it could be said *this moment speaks*," he rose the notebook up with enthusiasm as he spoke, lifting what looked like an old travel brochure from the bookmarked page, "There *is* no answer!" he shouted to the class in his most grasping voice, "Only the answer *is!*"

3

8:32 am - Sunday

The morning had began, but nobody seemed to mind, it was deep and dark, the hour meant nothing compared to the sky, which now dropped snow as if it had been banished from the heavens.

The news had said the evening before that it would be dropping three to four inches an hour for most of the morning.

It was advised that nobody would go out, but nonetheless the conference on *Academic Responsibility in the Digital Age* was still ongoing at Hillbrandt College, for most of the academics had been flown in, and today was the last day of the event, in which the culminating efforts of the discourse developed throughout the week would be organized and put to workshop.

T had submitted a request to be approved as part of the officiating panel which sorted through the materials and efforts of discourse accumulated throughout the conference.

Essentially, each panel throughout the week would have a stenographer whose primary task was capturing the critical narrative of the panel as it *occurred*, so that it could be said *what was said*, specifically as it related to the panel's collective materials.

This was something the College had recently started doing through the validated efforts of the continued learning groups established throughout the town of Vedici, the home of Hillbrandt College, which resoundly had a concomitance of around four to seven thousand participants for the continued learning group in any given year.

Usually the town residents who have returned after venturing out, usually after attending Hillbrandt, seek to continue learning about what is going on in the academic community, because it gives them a *cultured relevance*, one they don't feel like they can attain anymore from the mainstream culture, too much of television had become serialized formulas bent on taking focus of the prime time, *it's just a competing fanfare of circus horns seeking to get the most attention*, they would say to sound educated, and then continue to watch it and talk about it, *so they went to the continued learning groups*, that way when they weren't talking about television they could be talking about other things that made themselves feel *relevant*, ugh, how much this word was being tossed around, as if it was a necessary aspect of a commodity, to *be* the thing that people are currently buying, as if it is important for everyone in the economy to all be doing the same things at the same time, there are really only two ways that can go, either some few people are getting really rich, or a lot of people are losing money, and some few people are probably still getting rich, I

13

call it the chicken wings during the super-bowl scenario, imagine, what would happen, if one year there was something that made the chickens not up to count for all the slaughter that is consumed in just a few hours, the great sacrifice to the poultry gods, no better fitting homonym for the game, for what better thing to do than eat, and thus what do most people all agree upon if not the food, because the game itself is always supposed to be a point of dissension, that way it's interesting no matter what, quite like those reality shows everyone is now watching, and always talking about, *I mean did you see what happened*, hah, oh, hmmm.....where was I...where am I....oh right, the chicken wings during the super bowl, now imagine if there were not enough chickens, and imagine that nobody wanted to believe it, I mean come on it's the super bowl how could they not have enough chickens, man, the stores wouldn't believe it, managers would be telling their employees to lie, to say, *no, no, don't worry, it's coming, we will have them before the game, just make sure you come then*, and then they have the stores close on the day of the game, man imagine, those managers thinking they just avoided some rabble rousing towards the store, but really they got the whole neighborhood angry, together in the parking lot at the grocery store, with nothing to agree upon except their love for chicken wings and the super bowl, except there are no chicken wings, and what is a super bowl without chicken wings, now they are driving to other stores, going to other neighborhoods, where the faces are less friendly, and the managers just as stupid, and you got whole counties starting to act amuck just before the big game, when now you got people from different towns looking at each other realizing they drove too far to get back in time, and now they are at another parking lot, across state borders with a smug patriots fan telling you Donovan McNabb just threw an interception in the end zone, and the laughing really gets to you so you start to tell them to shut up, and then someone else says it was nullified by a penalty, so you start laughing back, telling them that McNabb hasn't thrown a red zone interception all season, that he was money in the endzone, and that the eagles were going to win, then something more was felt, that the chicken wings didn't matter, it's more about the game, about beating the patriots, and these smug fans laughing, who now start laughing even harder as you start walking back to your car in that ShopRite parking lot, the one, lone parking lot lamp towering twenty feet high, misty rain in the air up by it, as the light cast a perfect lane back towards their car, them standing there laughing, to tell you McNabb just threw another interception, while you start running up to tackle the one that was still dumb enough to be standing outside of the car, as the ones who weren't hop out to start beating you in the back, but there are still other fans in the parking lot, still other chicken wing searchers, and searchers nonetheless of something entertaining, and they run over and realize their purposes have never been more clear in life, that they have fists and they can use them, for there are clearly those here who deserve them and those who will back them up, how in this one ShopRite parking lot a war broke out, a whole group of people from different places, some who probably *did* know each other, punching and kicking, shouting profanities interlaced with sports trivia, while a light mist and a lone, lamp illuminated them, and somewhere the patriots and eagles were scoring no touchdowns, and nobody anywhere was excited by the game, or the chicken wings their county did have that year, and nobody else had to spend the night in jail for being pinned as the instigator of the whole damn thing, my fault, man, it was the damn chickens.

T tossed around in bed, the soft alarm could do nothing to rouse the mind, wait, man, I gotta get up.

Yet through those darkened minds there existed something more, something on top of themselves, perhaps a demon, or a spirit nonetheless, which imposed upon them this desire to not see the day, to keep into sleep, this sleep, how it was beckoning them forth, deeper and deeper into themselves, a deepness all too becoming of itself, how it became its own form, a lost sense, unknown, what is sleep when I am asleep, what am I when I am asleep, where does my mind go, how does it lay there as if calm in the valley of my thoughts, as rumbling the wind always beckons and shouts and screams from fights past arise and take me over, so that only sleep is all I know, this dark home of my soul, how I beckon myself here willingly, to live deep in this pain, to feel it constantly, to remind myself that *it is real*, not for suffering, no that is what T keeps telling me, *that I love the suffering*, but because *it is me*, as much as I want to avoid it, as much as I take my mind out of itself, and into those bodies that are not mine, into those roles and ways of speaking, *uh excuse me*, *what did you just say*, ah, *I cannot believe you said that, no you need to tell us what preposition first before we even consider you human enough for us to process what you are saying, not because we don't think you are not human, no we stopped believing that long ago, promise, here are some more opportunities,* and *new beginnings*, new ventures, venture capital, robots, robots, robots, the world is going to end, the world is going to end, because of that damn machine in the corner of the room, that machine we spent a summer's rent on just to be running in and out of the apartment for new jobs, not to use it, *got to get to the web*, T said, *got to use the word processor, there is opportunity here, a chance to switch positions in this world*, hah, how, how could you switch positions with them, they are already machines, hah, they can't even hear what I am saying unless I *use the right prepositions*, they are the word processors, man I don't have time for these dreams, they making me soggy-headed, wait, it's morning, it's so dark, T, where you going, T...

"T, baby, come on go back to sleep," Marla rolled over to look towards the now risen T.

"No, love, I gotta get up today, today is a big day", T said shaking off the sleep still billowing.

"You don't want to go back to sleep with me, rest in these covers?" Marla said with a smile, flashing the covers open, as her rapturous energy and the comfort of the bed radiated out a signal of sleep drawing T forth...

"...No, love...I said...I need to get up today, I just have to...I know it...today is going to be a big day" T said while wiping away the sleep, and stretching before the frame of the door.

The frame a cherry wood, enclosing the rather tall port that they had filled with hanging blue beads, a cascading entrance into a room that sat only their bed, a small desk, and a dresser, with a closet stuffed to suffocation and a hanging bar only hanging on because the clothes are holding *it* up.

"You want to go sit by the phone, again?" Marla tried to sit up against the pillow but fell quickly back down into a sleeping position.

Her eyes gently closed as she began to smile, as if the sleep she was having was whispering sweet nothings into her ear.

"That's right," T said looking through the dresser for some clothes, how on days like this T wished there was more strategy when it came to professional outfits, but always outfits were an attempt at deconstructing the profession, finding the aspects that were the fashion of the role, embracing it, and then avoiding that which were its ancient history, the heritage that lived through collars buttoned tight, and jackets well-hemmed with multiple fabrics, the value that goes into shoes, too much, too much for somebody most usually talking to books and through books.

"They ain't gonna call, you know..." T started to leave the room without acknowledging Marla. "What, you think they still want you? It is the last damn day for them to call, and it ain't going to happen, what do you want to spend the whole day out there, in the cold, in that green chair by the phone, looking out the window like a sad puppy, hoping they going to call, well they ain't it don't matter what you want they ain't calling..." She may have continued talking to herself, it is unclear if it is her yelling or her sleep-self has emerged.

"It don't matter what anybody *wants*," T yelled back towards the room, now sitting in the cold, green chair by the phone, looking outside as a small puppy plays on the front lawn of their neighbor, whom happened to already shovel the drive this morning, and has his three kids playing around the yard, throwing snowballs, before his mansion of a house, "life is not a battle of competing wants, sure I *want* to sleep, and sure they dont *want* me, sure, I could sit here by the phone all day *wanting* to be called, but I could just as well think of something else I *could want* and then *want* that, life is not about *wants*, damnit, it is about life being lived, and each day rising through the *wants* to become who I am supposed to *be*."

T started back towards the room to get dressed, now determined to go out.

"Well, you know what T, some of us don't just want because other people are *not wanting* us, some of us just don't live that life each day, we ain't waking up thinking about Frank Miller or whomever it is living next door that's *wanting* less and *wanted* more than us, we waking up next to our demons, sitting on our chests, telling us we are weak, reminding us of all the ways the world has shown us that pain, and letting that pain be right here, just because the sun ain't, so I am going back to sleep, not just because I *want* but it is because what *I need*, what I am *made to* need, because I don't have no place to fight, no place to exorcise these demons, *they are just my pain*."

She tossed around in the covers, several times as if she was burrowing into a soft bed of dirt, to hide further from the day, and forget it all away.

T looked from the closet back to the mound of covers, still able to notice the curves of a body known so well.

"You know that's what I am fighting, you know I am here to say we all deserve the right to fight our demons, and we can't be just seeing education as a passive and selective activity...*you* know that, and you know you are always stronger than your pain, that it is *your pain*, and thus there ain't anybody better to conquer it than you."

T pulled-on a red sweater, over a deep green, buttoned shirt, and quickly jumped into some brown pants, slipping on the cheap socks Marla bought at the department store saying that the more that come in a package the better a deal, something T thought instead only related to the thread count, T's head shook, *more negative thoughts, the sleep wanting to pull me back into itself, nothing comfortable enough for a day of struggle*, and so T stepped into a different posture, one which allowed the chest to expand the lungs to breathe, so that arms were not hanging down, so that the back was actually being supported by the legs rather than falling into itself, that said I am here because I choose to be not because I was made to exist, looking at the standing mirror that sat in the corner between the closet and the bed at a solemn face, alone in its fixity, for T knew not it, not the expression, not the mind, not the soul looked through the face, rather it hung, ready and poised to meet those outside, to snap with electricity into a smile and a greeting, to meet each statement with reassurance and support, to show all that *you* got what *they* were saying, that was the only way T knew how to convince people, to show them that their theory had lead itself astray into a domain of non-fixity, only to be asked why it is you're so interested in these things, why does it matter whether who said what in other disciplines, why would Logic need to be brought into Literature Studies, it was none of your concern, nothing T could really know, how could T understand, man, T, how could T, they'd say it right to my face, not with their words of course, but with their faces...a face lost, lost again in the mirror, T had fallen back into a stupor, but stood up straight, again, to shake the sleep one last time, and quickly grabbed a bag before running out the door.

4

April 20, 2012

A new day has begun, and somewhere, in some house, perhaps nearby, perhaps farther than is comfortable, though I am sure he wouldn't notice, a man wakes in his rather drab house, one sloped roof, caressing a fortress of a support wall on the opposite side, a house pythagoras may have been jealous of, for it is a truer realization of his theorem than he ever was living, how this man bounces from side to side, tumbling from his lofted cot to his slotted shower, down his circulating stairs into one lone room with a small toilet, enclosed on three sides with the shower above it on the mid-level, so that the ceiling is just too short to be able to stand up straight, and the one hanging light will get you if you are looking at eye level, so instead of much on the walls, there is really just a T.V. on the floor, a stack of newspapers, a brown corduroy reclining chair, and a small green table with a lone chair and dish rag hung over it, the table is under the light which is located exactly, unknowingly of course, at the center of the room so that upon the exit from the stairs, which sits in the farthest angle from the door, your eyes would go temporarily blind from looking right at the light which intersects a

straight line to the entrance of the building, sitting at
the mid-section of the wall, which in turn opens
directly to the table, chair and lone T.V., which
interestingly enough, sits at the mid-section of the
wall which would be considered the hypotenuse, so
that upon entrance you only see the T.V., the stack of
papers, the chair, the blinding light in the center, and
then in the only right angle sits a kitchenette which
has above it the lofted bedroom, which holds exactly
one dresser and a standing mirror, with the shower
right before the entrance to the stairs, and the toilet
greeting you as well at the base, it would be easy to
imagine, that with the routine of living here, this man
enters unknowingly of where it is that he sleeps, for it
is unseen, thus his body goes towards the kitchen *or*
the T.V. for it is impeded by the table in addition to the
light, and there he, consumes, always ignorant of the
other, for the table and the lamp impede the vision of
each other, and under the light it is too bright to look
anywhere but down, and then there is the bathroom
which anywhere outside of is blinded by the light, and
when you go upstairs the light is the result of a small
candle that probably is changed once a month and lit
only for the few moments it takes to climb into the
bed, you'd have to imagine *then*, waking up, to the
complete darkness, to shower in the dark, and change
in the dark, to come downstairs, and then only see the

room for an instant before the light is lit again so that breakfast can be made and something else too in the bathroom, and then it's around the revolving obelisk of incandescence, subidiving all being into the resolute, alone, mis-guided, singular task, to get into the car, this one with a fittingly sloped roof, from a dent perhaps from a moment of frustration towards its roof from both the interior and the exterior, perhaps at different times, to driving on this pothole filled road on a street which looks like the town that once held it perhaps was deleted from the simulation, for there are complete lots which look untouched since the days of yore, and homes mis-matching aesthetic eras by vast distances of time, and the solemn accompaniment of other activity, as no one seems to leave the house, perhaps their participants were also deleted from this trial of inanity, for our lone man ventures out, unknowing, perhaps not caring, perhaps knowing something else, perhaps knowing nothing at all, maybe not even his own name.

There the freeway arrives and back into society and civilization he emerges, slightly unseenly for his clothes mis-match from the dark, and his face still has food on it as he rushed out without considering to wash upstairs in the slotted shower, and his car burps emissions every so often too, as his axel is slightly bent and one tire looks like it gave up long ago considering to fall off and instead is proud of its accomplishment as being the only tire on the road at such an angle, and there he drives towards the city which has beckoned him, one he has never been to before, which houses a college in the rolling hills, where a professor has pissed off a lot of people, and he is there to figure out what he can prove is wrong and settle it, or at least that is what his boss told him when they hired this man as an investigator, one instigated under the grand premises of a supreme injunction, yet somehow, the prosecution was able to secure for itself the right to an independent investigator given the pretenses that this supreme injunction was still contained within the confines of the collegiate judicial system, only symbolically aligned in effort and according by federal mandate, but for the most part is its own, lone outpost dictating how it is that any should live in accordance with the life prescribed from outside.

That of course, and the town itself, which seemed to hold a great regard for the College, at least that is what this man was told, and he seemed to think it was a nice town because when he passed the hardware store, and started driving up the hill his frown became a flat-line.

Then when he passed the sign that mentioned a chocolatier he thought to himself he might stop there on his way out of town, and he also noticed that some people were walking on the sidewalk, one gentleman standing in a doorway gave a hearty wave to another walking down the block.

The hill up to the College was steep.

When he got to the top he turned into the parking lot, he pulled into a spot but, no, he decided to reverse and park in the spot opposite to it, *neat*, the spot he didn't park in was *2B*.

When he got towards the entrance of the school he pulled a leaf off of one of the trees, the tree flung backwards in a chaotic movement to gain stability.

When he got inside he went to the first office there, it said *Campus Security*, and he figured they would know what the situation was that was going on, at the school, that or who would, his boss didn't give him very much information.

"My boss didn't give me very much information," he said.

He didn't greet anyone, he just walked in and said it.

Nobody responded so he said it again, "My boss didn't give me very much information."

It is not that he said it with more emphasis or emotion, he just said it, I don't know if he thought...er...uh, nevermind.

"Yes, how can I help you," said a nice young woman behind the desk, her name placard read *Mabel*, "what is it that you need?"

"I am here for the investigation, is there a lead officer around that I can speak to?" The man said back not changing the position of his eyes from when he first walked in the room, well probably not since he looked at the chocolatier sign, but who's counting, I stopped a while ago, seriously, it's maddening.

"I am the only person in this office, *sir*," Mabel said with emphasis to get the man to look at her, "We here at Hillbrandt pride ourselves on the accessibility of our faculty and administration, so as *head* of campus security it is that my desk is right here when you walk in, I have no secretary," she said now a little unsure, with her hand reaching under the desk ever so slightly, "what investigation are you here for?"

"The one about the teacher, the teacher who pissed everyone off!" The man said out of disdain, not for Mabel, or the teacher, really, just because disdain had been a feeling imparted on this man when he was a young boy, he didn't know why then and he didn't know why it came back up now, but when it did he didn't question it, he just let it back through to the surface.

"Well...*uh*...I think you might mean the professor who incited many students to start rioting, *yes*, unfortunate incident indeed, the professor in question had actually been a part of our cherished community for almost five years, it seems like some of the research had produced a lapse in the professor's mind, *analysis paralysis* they say, and it took over the lectures and caused some of the students to panic, they had been too stressed because of the semester, *anyhow*, it is not me that you are supposed to meet with," she lifted her hands back onto the table to pull out a file folder, "interestingly enough, I was asked by the Provost and Dean of the

College, *same person*, to hand this to you and take you to a room to do your work.

Our esteemed Professor Gershom is off on sabbatical, and has a perfect office for you to sit and look over the files."

The man was taken to the office and promptly sat down and started reviewing the files.

They seemed to be out of order, he was not sure, but very much felt like someone was playing a prank on him.

He got up to go out of the office when the office next door abruptly opened and invited him in, they apparently knew his name.

"*Raca*, please, enter!"

5

June 6th,

    the night before the trial:

"Thank you Professor Gershon, for joining me here, it is an honor."

"It is actually, *Gershom*, but yes, how is it that I can help you today?

"Well, then I stand corrected, it is a *gershom,* well, thank you again."

"Did you prepare any questions for me?"

"Of course!"

"Can you please read them?"

"Certainly, okay first, how long have you been a professor at Hillbrandt College?"

"Hmm, let me think, I graduated in sixty-four from Copper's, then I completed my doctorate twelve years after that, at Hillbrandt, and I started officially as a professor a year after that."

"So a couple decades you are saying."

"Well actually, no, it has been thirty-six years."

"Okay so three decades, got it."

"Three and a half."

"Got it.

Okay, now, please, next question, how long did you know Professor Cinotau before the *incident*?"

"Which incident, you could be more specific."

"Which incident? There have been several?"

"Which are you referring to?"

"Well, I am not...er...uh, Professor, please, I am asking the questions here.

There was an incident in question in which, Professor Cinotau is being put on trial, for the classroom riot that had occurred just a few months ago.

If there is another incident, I am sorry, but I am not asking about that, I don't know what that is."

"What that *is*? How could you not, Cinotau is a thief!"

"What are you talking about, a thief?"

"Yes! A thief! Cinotau defrauded the whole academic community, with *my theories*, everyone thought that Cinotau was some type of prodigy, because of my *theories*, they gave away a tenured position that my niece was supposed to get, because of it, believe that, my theories!"

"Okay, Professor, I am sorry to hear your theories were taken, were you ever able to get them back?"

"You don't get it."

"I get that you are very *frustrated.*"

"Just the word I was thinking."

"Okay, so you are saying that Professor Cinotau is a fraud? That the theories that caused the student revolt are rightfully yours?"

"Yes that's cor...wait no!

What *are you saying*, Cinotau incited those students because of radical belief, and *disdain* for the whole institution, ever since that smug face came in here spouting all sorts of knowledge from different disciplines, as if it was some feat to be multidisciplinary, as if it didn't mean that you just skirted through every obligation, never having to commit yourself to some history or narrative you didn't want to but had to because everything moved *through it*, no, just coming in here plucking theories from here and there, I am surprised I am the only one who ever said anything, I am sure other theories and work was stolen, probably stolen by that unhinged mind, taking all sorts of *poetic license*, reconstructing them so they don't mean what they were supposed to, they don't mean anything to what we've already done, encouraging these students towards the progressive, as if they didn't live on the bluest spot on the whole planet, of course there are big speckles of red, don't get me wrong, but, oh where was I, that Cinotau, took the theories to convince all those students to revolt!"

"Professor, that is a serious accusation you are bringing forth, do you have any proof?"

"Proof! Proof! Cinotau took my proofs! Look at any of the classroom lectures, the notes, I bet you can find something there."

"I am sorry Professor, I have reviewed those documents myself and I didn't see your name written on any of them, so I am not sure if Professor Cinotau has your theories."

"How can you be this dull?"

"Hey, let me remind you, that although we are on the campus of the College you are employed, I have been asked by the administration *and* the town to be here, so again, *I am the one asking the questions.*"

"Then ask, or are we done?"

"Well, I want to help you out Professor Gershon, I really do, so can you tell me *when* your theories were taken?"

"You know, you know, actually, that question would be meaningless in most other plagiarism scenarios, but in this one there might actually be something here.

So, about five years ago, when I think the incident in question, *first* occurred, I was on leave for sabbatical in Italy, I had a very important theory that I was working on, and by mistake I had left the notebook and some papers in my office, it was really terrible, I went to Italy to work but I had nothing to work on, *and nothing to do.*

Anyway I digress, during that trip there was a conference at the school, which is when this all started, there had been some big commotion or whatnot, and I had overheard from one of these students, they emailed me actually, emailed me outright with the name of my theory in the message, asking me *if I could explain it to them*!

The audacity of some people.

Anyway, the student wasn't from here, some other school or another, and I didn't respond, because I was on sabbatical, but when I returned I figured it must have been during that conference.

My notebook was still out on the desk, and so were the papers I had forgotten, but they had been moved in a way that I would have never placed them.

I asked myself, at the time if it was me, and I was confused, because one page in my notebook *had* been bookmarked, and it was the exact theory the student had emailed me about.

You know, I always figured that the students had snuck into my office *looking for the theory*, but it may have been something more insidious.

Now that I am thinking about it, there was a paper towel on top one of the books in the shelf, it had this brown crust on it, it was gross, multiple shades of brown, I didn't want to know what it was so I had someone come clean it, but I had forgotten about that.

You know, I think that they let someone stay in my office during that conference, and that whoever was there stole my theory then, and I think, *you know*, who better to encourage some somebody to sneak into a Professor's office, you know to really revolt, by taking the theory...sounds like something Cinotau would have done don't *you think*?"

You know, now that I *really think* about it, I remember people saying over email, you know when I checked when I came back, so it was months later that I had gotten back to those emails, but nonetheless, they were talking about how somebody was attempting to get in the conference but nobody on the Continued Learning Committee would permit it, and *that* I can confirm, they have only gotten worse with their intra-politics, you could do a case study on their growth and you'd might have something to say about those super PACs, because the way information is handled in those things is basically the same, anyway, that's too much, let me say, I don't think *somebody* was supposed to be there...do you see what I am getting after?"

"Wow.

I can see why you are a professor, *clearly*, but you'd make an incredible investigator."

"Excuse me?"

"Or even a judge."

"Well, you know I had considered it at one point.

I was always a student of letters, and was just not sure if I was wanting to use that wit on the page or the bench, but ultimately I decided it would be better to be able to say what you want everywhere, and not just when the law is on your side."

"Well said!"

"So, are you going to investigate that conference, perhaps you can figure out who was responsible for letting people past the gate?"

"Great idea!"

6

Third Class

"Okay class, today we are going to do something different, as you all know, it is a tradition at this school to assimilate the culture of the students into the community of academics, thus we do not always want to belabor you to the point of erudition, but instead allow you to explore the other ways that you can *be* an academic, today we are going to the bi-monthly faculty social," Professor Dillinger said to a group of students that looked as enthused as *you* probably do, but really these things are fun, I promise, Professor Dillinger thought to himself.

The class is about fifteen feet by six feet with a twenty foot ceiling, I only say this because it is an odd shape.

However, because of its high ceilings it is permitted to have large windows, which really make up for it, because there is a stunning lake view through those windows, the students look right and *right there* is another student, I mean for the students on the left, for the students on *the right*, there is a lake view.

The class sits students two by two all the way to the front.

Their names are James, Mallory, Marna, and Timothy...no wait it is Tommy, I got to remember that.

Since it was still the ending days of summer, the class was fortunate enough to attend one of the faculty socials *that are outside*, which for some reason makes all the difference, probably because of the walls not being there and everything, *they keep in the stuffiness.*

And, for even further benefit, this faculty social being outside, in the last days of summer, was selected to be down at *Bender's Beach*, that hip, new spot down by the lake, where that stunning view comes from, so the students will get to ride a shuttle down the hill to the lake, I am sure they will enjoy *that.*

By now the students hadn't finished gathering up their things, it wasn't that they had so many things that *needed* to be out, but they had a lot of things that were out, on the small little tables they each share, so that six different paper stacks need to be re-color-organized before getting zipped back up, in the protective paper folder, before being put into the special compartment in the backpack, oh, *it has a buckle.*

"Are other classes going to be there?" Marna asked walking towards the front of the room with her bag on her back, the other students following after, except for Timothy who had stopped to tie a shoe.

"Well, whatever other classes *meet* at this time, so I don't really know what that means about *who* will be there," Professor Dillinger said as he opened the door before holding for students to exit, "but there is going to be a handful of faculty, and some may have even thought they were *supposed to bring bathing suits!*"

8

9:15 am - Sunday

The car is making that noise again.

It clicks loud in the back, like the latch on the rear hatch is loose, clicking in and out, while the other latch holds on for dear life keeping the tailgate from opening while driving on the road, it really *should* get fixed, but right now it just clicks.

T pulls out of the detached garage sitting just to the right of the house.

Click.

T built it a few years back for mornings just like this, when there was snow but T had to go, no time to clean, just time to drive, reverse, looking at the side view mirror while the house sits in the background.

Click.

It is a small red brick, two-level, traditional colonial roofing and sides, with a small walk in the front that splits and goes around to a backyard, but right now it looks like it just goes into the sky, it is still snowing pretty heavily, I cannot even see past the maple tree that sits between the house and the one next-door, click.

The rest of the houses on the block have similar looks and feels, nobody really has updated much in a while, except for the neighbor across the street, who T now sees down the street, walking with his three kids back from sledding, click.

Click, as T passes the youngest one throws a snowball at the dad, and he laughs it off while giving the middle one a noogie, the oldest continues to pull the sled, mom must have a warm meal ready for them because you can see his face is forgetting about the cold and beginning to think about the opportunities his day has, which area of his possessive reach can he access, how open the world is to a youth with possibility, click, with opportunity, man if only everyone had access to cable television, and computers, sleds, click, dads who laugh all the time, big houses, moms who love cooking meals just at the right time, man, if only everyone lived that way, click, maybe then the world would just work out the way everyone thinks it could, click, maybe then there would be some pace to things, maybe there wouldn't be so much confusion, click, and pushing and fighting and traffic...traffic on the highway, T is stuck behind a big dump truck, drunk, dropping salt onto the road, there are about six cars slugging behind, you can tell some of the later ones just joined because they are trying to weave around the lane of cars only to quickly pull back realizing that the road on the other side is temporarily rendered hazardous by the outpouring of salt from the truck.

T stays in line with the few and solemn still out making it to work or wherever it is they have to go on a day, a morning like this, click, probably already dropped four inches since T woke up this morning, the car just started to warm and the seat is getting hot, old car, but has seat warmers, click, funny how some things don't become standard and keep getting peddled as new, T passes the auto-dealer on the right, click, it's right before the gas station and that old diner T tried going to a few times but the way the waitresses addressed the regulars made it feel like I was intervening on some old tradition that should have ended centuries ago, click.

There is another route I can take, bending off the highway onto the on-ramp, onto a bigger highway, click, fortunately enough it's already been plowed and salted, less cars, but still some traffic considering how much snow is falling.

T reaches for the radio.

A classical guitar starts playing, and everything seems right.

The cars keep moving steadily, and there is not much time being felt, the mind drifts into itself, unfolding thoughts as the body continues driving and T's soul is nourished by the music, T lets the music unpack all of the terrors the night before brought and the horrors left in the body, remembered only as emotion in the morning, how so constant this cycle was for T, searching through days for something that would never arrive, how first T became convinced it would never make sense to pursue these things, to go after a College position, T had not much right to be a teacher anywhere let alone at Hillbrandt, they didn't usually work with those that had not already been indoctrinated through their system, the best six years of learning a mind could ever encounter they'd say, and then they'd encourage the whole town to keep sending their children there so seventy-five percent of the population was from the town itself, an absurd factory of delusion T sometimes thought, but also the best place T had found that would receive the work, this work, the one in the bag on the leather-upholstered seat next to T.

The guitar stops playing and now some string-instruments are starting a quick melody, the grey interior of the car starts to radiate with the sun's light that is now just breaking through the clouds, click.

The highway has pulled out from where the stores and businesses had been and now is surrounded by trees, the cars are moving faster, despite the road seemingly more hazardous, every so often a tree lets a load of snow fall from its branches and a large cloud is summoned by the wind that sends the snow towards the road, the brass and wind instruments are entering into the symphony, click, slowing the tempo, as the snow is just barely reaching the cars as mist, because now the sun has squarely decided it will remain alight, as the snow seems to settle down and the darker clouds had been receding east for some time now, T looks up from wherever being lost in thought had left the eyes to rest to dart unknowingly towards an exit coming up.

The car quickly veers, cutting over two lanes, and off, as the third movement of the symphony comes into full rhythm, T goes from the highway onto a two-lane road that continues to follow the same path as the highway, but now is deeply entrenched in the trees so that the sun is flickering through the branches, and keeping T in a stupor as T focuses, the horns blowing, one-two-three, dark-light-dark-light, snow-mist-sun, on-and-on, for two miles while T's eyes remain fixedly on the road so as not to inadvertently pull the wheel in an off-direction because of the flashing light, as the string instruments return to a stressful staccato, plucking fast and hard, and the rest of symphony plays their respective parts through to a loud clash, click.

And the road opens again, the trees have cleared, the entrance of a small town, the radio switches to a jazz percussion break as a host of a new show begins to talk.

9

May 13, 2012

For the past three weeks, *Raca*, has been investigating the case of our dear Professor. Here is what he has learned since the beginning of the case:

Professor Cinotau

Professor of Letters & Motions

Hillbrandt Ʊ College

—extremist on technology
  —>advocating a strategic approach
      at dismantling capitalistic
      structures of opinion

—deluder of students
  —> producing erratic seminar
      causing students to revolt

Was there more that could be written, probably, was there more that *should be written*, yes definitely, but Raca now had more bosses, with more orders and some of those included not disclosing very much about what it is that Raca was thinking in regards to the case, until the trial that is, so as to prevent the defense from catching wind of what it was that the prosecution was planning to say before the jury, they asked Raca if he would have any trouble to stop himself from disclosing his thoughts before the trial, I think they were serious, they offered to set him up with accomodations somewhere, somewhere nice even, and he said, "No place like home."

For the past two nights he has been watching a television-rerun-athon.

Dallas was being revived, and even though Raca was only nine years old when it went off the air, he tells people he was there when J.R. was shot *and killed*, and they usually assume he was old enough judging by his appearance, but they aren't thinking about more than that, he himself isn't sure why he looks the way he does, at some point he stopped paying attention to the changes his body was making in the mirror, you know once he had found the routine of shaving and washing that he liked, his barber really never said much, or at least *little*, and would always turn Raca away from the mirror to face the bathroom wall.

Speaking of bathroom walls, well, lack thereof, you know, that open door-policy, forever enshrined by his three-walled stall, right next to his kitchen no less, and he rigged his ventilation in the bathroom, oh yes, he installed his own ventilation in the stall, anyway...he rigged it to push the air through to the shower, with a small opening he cut in the linoleum frame, so that 'it' could go out of the hole and into the vent for the shower, he was actually proud of this and would have shown it off to anybody that visited his home...if anybody ever did visit his home.

Anyway, there he sits, or stalls, I don't know, I am not *really* looking, but nonetheless he has been starting to get very inspired by his television watching, the way he usually does, lost in their *mystique*, he says privately to himself every so often, how he feels himself walking to the bathroom sometimes during commercial breaks, the last line said still reverberating through his cheeks, more lively than he is at any other time, but he doesn't notice, there is no mirror in the bathroom, that's upstairs getting fogged up, oh okay he is done.

He now is sitting at the table, it seems he has pulled that same manila folder out from somewhere, I haven't really been able to figure it out, because usually he gets it *after* going to bathroom, and I can't watch the environmental rights violation that is his repeated failure to walk right next-door, or next-lack-thereof-door, to the sink and wash his hands, but no, never hear it, only that folder *gets procured* from somewhere, I don't even know if he is actually hiding it or just doesn't have anywhere to keep it and where he is keeping it *is* where he keeps things, if he keeps anything, really, it is quite incredible how his wardrobe somehow remains the same exact level of disheveled throughout the week, it is actually remarkable, this *I have* been paying attention to, okay get this, he has four shirts, one with buttons, two with collars, one red, one green, and two white, you'd think okay, right so six shirts, seven days, he must have to repeat those shirts one and a half times on average, so he could select the not most dirty ones and then be relatively clean each week so long as the shirts were cleaned twice a month, right, not a bad guess, but like I said, one red, one green, and two white, the two white being two undershirts, the red and green *being* the two collared-shirts, so the red and green are repeated three to four times *a week*, fortunate for the red and green, because it gives the two white shirts time to air out, on the three days he doesn't *work*, is what he calls it, driving back to the school, driving past the chocolatier, and *having to stop there*, because the traffic always makes it harder to park on the way back, so that he just *has to* sit at the french bakery and have his chocolate bar over his baguette with a small hot chocolate in an espresso cup, *to do it like the Belgians do*, he said offhandedly to the barista, probably because he was feeling relatively chum after passing the fish market.

Okay so it's Sunday, I can tell because a white shirt is on, *only*, and it's already pretty dark brown under the armpits, well anyway he has opened the folder, and what I recorded, up *there*, earlier is what is still written, he reads over it, and then does that thing where he exhales and massages his temples, because he thinks it clears stress, because he saw it on T.V., but I don't even know what he is stressed about, seriously, I have tried to penetrate that head many times, and I know the language is bad, but really, I used even the bad language, nothing got in, he doesn't seem interested by me, well, anyway, enough of that, shh, he is *thinking*, it needs to be very quiet in here, I think so he finally hears the silence that is his own mind and moves on in interest of some food, thinking he is *cracking the case*, he says ironically to himself when he either grabs a beer from his perennial thirty-rack or those walnuts he now eats, *since he has been hired as an investigator*, with the statuette he got from his Aunt Miriam, when he was seventeen, so that he'd have one for his own, you know, incase the robots *did* take over.

I'd speculated whether or not the pages afterwards, other than the one I already recorded, are blank or not, but I was too fearful to check, in case it was that it just held his name and birthdate, until one day he lifted the top page, and the next page had his first name underlined next to his birth year, perhaps the jury was still out on the last name and day.

I don't know why I try most of these days, there is no way he is going to change his mind, if he doesn't even have a mind operating to notice change.

Really, I know I have gotten cynical, but I am not calling him stupid, stupidity is relational, it is situational, it is momentary, this is abjection to the meaning of life itself, I don't know if he gets too frustrated thinking about anything, like he always is, *frustrated*, but I also think that at one point he just liked the fact that people always said he was so frustrating, that he *liked* being frustrating for a period of time, and that last part of himself that had any resolve to be cordial within a group, that is, in the way *he is himself* rather than just the pleasantries he still finds himself automatically saying, dissipated completely and he either stopped caring or noticing, like his appearance in the mirror, if he looked, it shifted and adapted to this word *frustration*...frustration with what *really*, in the grand scheme of things, what do *you really* have to be frustrated about, and to be *so* frustrated that your car is the way it is, your life is the way it is, because of the moments and situations when you couldn't relate and frustration or *disdain* were all you knew so you allowed *those words*, those affects, to become you, to become your spirit, to become your personality, what say you!

"Erhmph," Raca said while scratching at his exposed buttocks, a few of the walnut shell-pieces had fallen through his lap and were pressed aggressively between the small chair and the...the Raca.

10

June 5th,
                two nights before the trial:

"So, your name is Melissa, right?"

"Yes that is correct."

"Okay, Melissa, I am going to ask you some questions, is that okay with you?"

"Yes, that is what I am here to do."

"Right!"

"Yeaah"

"Okay, so how...uh...did you meet Professor Cinotau?"

"Excuse me?"

"Oh! I am sorry, I mean, uh, I mean did you know Professor Cinotau?"

"Yes."

"What was your...uh...*opinion* of Professor Cinotau?"

"Professor Cinotau was nothing short of a revolutionary really, I know that is probably not the right word to use, right now of all times, but really, oh that was the wrong word, I don't think any of this is fair you know?"

"You don't?"

"No, not at all.

Professor Cinotau is a good person, plain and simple.

This is less about anything Professor Cinotau has done than what this school *does*."

"What do you mean?...I am sorry if I am being too invasive, I didn't mean to upset you."

"No it's okay, it's just that I think all of this is coming from somewhere else. It's just it doesn't make sense for all these students to revolt. It just doesn't make sense. I'm telling you, why would the students revolt, Professor Cinotau taught literature.

Something is fishy here!"

"You don't think there was a conspiracy, do you?"

"I don't know, maybe there was!

You should know you are the investigator."

"Me?

No, they don't tell me anything. Half the time I'm racking my brain looking for new leads but I don't have anywhere to go, but I love conspiracies, I mean, now that was the wrong word too...uh...I mean what do you think happened?"

"I think somebody had it out for Professor Cinotau, just think about it, the whole town basically hands itself off to itself, generation after generation.

Everyone here has their life written in the stars, and Professor Cinotau is like an asteroid coming in from out of the solar system, or better yet, like Pluto!

Poor pluto."

"Do you like looking at the stars?"

"Yes, actually, it is something I enjoy, but I think we are getting off-track."

"Right, okay, so you are saying that Cinotau is an outsider?"

"That's right, Professor Cinotau came out of nowhere basically, and shook the whole system up, they couldn't do anything about it too, the students love Professor Cinotau, and this town is made for its students.

What better way to push someone out then to get the best advocate for them, the students, to no longer be seen as credible in making their own decisions.

Quite a parent thing to do don't you think, but it must have been someone with motive.

That is what I think, you always have to find motive!"

"Yes, that is true!

You know, on *Law & Order*, they practically can't have an episode without motive!"

"You can't have a crime without motive!"

"Wow, you must be a philosopher."

"Me, no, no, I am an English teacher at Vedici High, I very much enjoy it there.

Did you have any more questions?"

"Many more que...er, uh, yes, many more questions."

"Okay, I am ready, what are they?"

"Oh, okay, so what do you think...would be...the motive, *if*...Professor Cinotau actually did do it?"

"I am sorry, I am not sure if I feel comfortable answering that, I don't think Professor Cinotau did do it."

"No no, I am just curious, because you seem to know a lot about *criminal intent*, so I was just wondering, just for me, here I'll turn the tape off...**[t**
                                    a
                                    p
                                    e

f
a
s
t

f
o
r
w
a
r
d
e
d]...there."

"Okay, well if *you* are just interested in the hypothetical, I think it could be possible that Professor Cinotau *did do it*, because if you consider it this way, a lot of the students at this school do get really passionate and excited about things in this world.

I'd imagine it would be hard not to, considering they are basically just a step from staying at the top of it for the rest of their lives or falling down the hill as they say, and that comes with both a lot of stress, but also *frustration* towards the stress.

When I was younger, I used to get very radical myself, actually, that is, I would believe myself *to be a radical*, and I would find the theories and arguments that most aligned what I was going through at the time, and it was a way for me to really feel like I had a voice.

Before, I used to feel like I could never tell anyone what I was thinking, that it was too wrapped up in my emotions and nobody would ever get me, or what I was talking about.

But something about just knowing *things,* made me feel so confident in myself, it was like I was changing overnight, with each book I read, I was able to see it immediately reflect in my world.

But sometimes, when we are feeling build-up, and stress, and we are so used to getting that type of feedback from our work, or support from our teachers, there is a dangerous domain that academics don't really talk about.

It is called the fanatic stage, and what happens is the person realized that what they were working on was not as profound as they thought it was, *and that really matters*, because half the battle is convincing other people, and you have to have confidence for that, so people sometimes start to believe what they want to believe, when they are looking for confidence.

It is possible that maybe some of Professor Cinotau's students had been feeling all the stress, and each year things are getting more and more competitive, trust me I see it at Vedici, and whereas it's the norm at this point and just discourages students when we don't perform as well as the previous year, at Copper's they treat it like sacrilege, or some great shame, the town really does, people reflect it to each other in the way they talk about things, and for kids so young!

Those kids end up at Hillbrandt, and you could imagine, not really knowing Professor Cinotau, except for the reputation, and thinking that the classroom is going to be just another facet of the Vedici streamline, from wealth to wealth, success to success, and to have a professor that *really* challenges you, in a way you have never been challenged before.

Either the students planned to revolt because of it, I wouldn't put that past them either, or they couldn't handle Professor Cinotau's class.

Which is a shame really, it is a learning *opportunity* to be in those classrooms...or it was one of the parents, for the same reason, that or like I said earlier it was a conspiracy.

But what do I know?"

"Thank you! That was quite exciting, I am curious now to think about these things before the trial, will you be there?"

"I am not sure, but I do neeeed to go, okay bye!"

II

"Today I *really* want to try something different," Professor Dillinger said, " I am going to read a quote from a book, *and I am not going to tell you which one*, but I want you to reflect on what you think it means as it relates to your experience in this class, *now*, again, this *is* coming out of context, so it will be helpful to try to identify the referents that you know, and then from there start to build a narrative of what you understand, all of course, as it relates to what is *happening*, so please, allow your mind to be free and open to everything, and for that we will do a freewriting exercise, please bring them up *here* when you are done."

The relationship between the electricity and the magnetism of the brain is what generates the frequency within the brain that aligns the body with the conscious field (akashic), the correspondence of this relationship to the mathematical understanding of electricity and magnetism provides the semantic bridge to understand how it is that consciousness is shaped and existent as a field within nature.

There is no particle density, or any relation to materiality as a concept of quantum entanglement, rather, consciousness is the possibility of a perspective existing, which in the mathematical sense, validly exists as the Imaginary, and it is the upper bound of this perspective existing that is infinitely containing all possible perspectives that *could exist*, as a relation between a body maintaining a relationality between electricity and magnetism and that body actually existing within the moment as it exists.

Thus we are able to fold back into the semantic bridge to extend the semiotic map capable of situating meaning-as-it-relates-to the correspondence of the individual consciousness, as defined by the locality of the body, and the phenomenal engagement of what it is *that is* happening, and the *there is* that could be said to be the possible perspective *that could exist*, which we usually call Narrative.

This is how reality entered metaphysics, it folded itself, through the human experience, and now, I've unfolded it.

12

10:32 am - Sunday

Hillbrandt sits, fittingly, on top of a hill, overlooking a lake.

The lake had been there forever, perhaps when the glaciers first receded through the area.

It was fresh-water with a twang only a mother could love, but the town loved its slight-putrid green water nonetheless, they would bathe in it, dance and play in it, roll around on its beaches, they said it was the lake that made the town, but T was convinced it was the town that made *the lake*, they must put some chemicals in it, because everyone in this town is usually raving mad, about this and that, screaming just because they see someone they know on the street, as if their mind has been lost in the winding maze of the internet they are all too common to be living in these days, that at first sight of another they are shocked that the world is still real, that them robots ain't taking over again, hah, the panic and excitement all riding through the same channels, and man they tell me sometimes I'm erratic, because I get excited about my ideas, and they tell me ideas can take you out far in the middle of the lake with no paddle and no way home, *analysis paralysis*, lose your mind you will, lose your sense, *why*, because I had no sense to begin with, nothing identifiable for them to latch onto, to categorize and place in their ever roving knowledge about what this and that is, *what the opinion is*, what the points are, the debate, which side says what, *and who is really right*, how common these dispositions were now, everyone, even the teenagers running into the Starbucks to jump and scream at their friends simply because they are buying a drink, man, *this excitement, bottle it up and sell me some*, says the executive, the dads watching all the young kids, being reminded and affirmed of their own youth, of this passive tunnel of becoming they have crafted through history, so that the world *is outside*, always outside, never constructing the inside, dammit, I missed my turn.

There is a long winding road about a mile or two from where you enter the town limits from the forest grove.

You have to turn right after the hardware store, it's the one with the scarecrow hanging on the corner of the porch filled with stacks of welcome mats and big-brown barrels holding rakes, shovels, and wiffle ball bats, or whatever have-you, the scarecrow is in the corner of the porch that juts right out onto the sidewalk, so that the scarecrow is sticking out just enough that you know its black-lacquer smile isn't worn from years of advertising service, but the occasional hand that slaps it as it swings into a brisk pace to start up the street from the parking lot just a block west, a tradition some would say, an odd one, that's certain, this overcoming of violence they like to decry in this town, how all the sports are ethical because they have outlawed anything that would cause a bruise, yet they do things like this, man, I'm telling you, give it time, give it time, the road bends about three times, each with its targeted zoning of commercial and residential, designed to make the town look more and more impressive as you rise the hill, Lake Boulevard they call it, even though you cannot access the lake from it, and you cannot see the lake until you get to the top of the hill, where it becomes College Road, anyway, here's the turn, got it, okay, that damn scarecrow there it is, how you doing this morning, man, that smile's looking great haha, look they even put mittens on the scarecrow because of the snow storm, huh I hope there will be parking.

T continues up the boulevard as the buildings on the right and left are a mix of vintage shops, holding the old clothes and furniture best for those who haven't shopped elsewhere yet and are close enough to their car to considering buying a pile of old sweaters perfect for the party season, it was december after all, or an antique grandfather clock, or is that a redundancy to say these days, hmm, I wonder if they have grandfather clocks on the internet, the road winds to the right before turning quickly around to the left and up, causing a faux-cul-de-sac where there is a five-mile-per-hour circle-lane, some additional zoning of parking, and a small gazebo in the center, all bringing you to view a small market square nested on the far side of the bend, within it are lazy-shops fit for window-shopping and all sorts of knick-knack searching, as they meander in either direction from the square at the base of the hill.

If you walk through the square you would be going toward Howard Street, which is the main road access to the square, usually never any parking unless you are lucky, right now it's probably not plowed yet, and too far from the college to comfortably walk, Howard runs east towards the lake, opens up to house more of the town-focused stores, with parking lots, like the grocery store, wine seller, and then progressively intersects about four or five avenues, that go north towards where they catch back up with Lake Boulevard, and south until they reach the forest grove, with about twenty different blocks that expand out once the road gets more level, to the north the split-level housing is built into the rising hill so that each block looks like a small cluster of oysters stuck to a jetty that sticks out from the water at low tide, most of the houses have big living rooms contained by glass panel walls, they don't seem to care if the neighbors can look in, usually they're in each other's business enough anyway, anyway, I got to stop getting so frisky towards these people, man, smile.

Now T is driving around the bend to head up the hill, the road here is mostly plowed, would have been perfect for sledding about four hours ago, that kid could have had his mom drive him here, then he'd really have something to be proud of, man sled this, not the hill down the street, man you got to do things with risk in them, you got to wake up early in the morning, take mom's car and sled the damn thing yourself.

Man, what am I saying, this is nonsense, I think I am just really anxious, they are probably just going to turn me away when I get there, come on focus on the road, the road goes about half a mile at an eight percent gradient with all sorts of speciality shops, cheese, cured meats, hydroponic produce, fish, all housed in swiss-looking shops with the big windows on the second levels where you know the shopkeepers are probably hoarding more cash than the banks, because most of *their* money is probably off-shore, or overseas, or *invested*, probably way more than they've got above the shops, but not bad shops really, with decent parking, only thirty-minute limits to make sure people aren't taking too long for their conversations, *hey Felix how the fish this week, oh the same they have always been Benjamin, hahah that's a good one Felix, anything for you Benjamin*, or something, something they say every week, well now they aren't in there, all the spots are empty, except for the snow that the last few passes of the plow have packed, that will sure make an angry Martha or Mary in a few hours, *how could you block my access to speciality mahi mahi for my Lost viewing party*, while Felix would be standing outside, looking for Benjamin, but not now, he's upstairs somewhere, sleeping behind those big windows which are covered in snow, looking just as peaceful as ever as a group of professors walk by the serene, calm, up the hill towards the College.

They should have taken the 161A bus rather than the 161, it's the one that takes them up the hill rather than just to the shopping center.

Usually you'd catch the bus out by the train station by the forest grove, and it would be a clear delineation at the end of the day who worked where, who took the train into the city to work at the cushy job, or whatever they called their dreams, cushy, priss, prass, prat, wasp, wisp wap, or whatever words they used to separate themselves, not because of fashion or anything of that standard, but just because they'd get in two lines at the end of the day, *A or not A*, and anybody would know, who was who, the not-A bus would take them to the base of the town, where all the houses were no more than 800K but no less than 500K, and the elementary school has a big jungle gym, but not a full-sized basketball court, so sometimes the kids from 'down the hill' go to Copper's up on MaCarthur Street, which is actually one of the streets that intersects Howard, but you have to go on the other side of Lake Drive, where it has a nested plateau, for foundation to house that massive gymnasium which has a skylight and an outdoor balcony overlooking the lake, probably for all the parents, but the kids don't know the difference, they rove around their extra and new wings, with biology and chemistry equipment, a small, functioning telescope, in a dome building at the north of campus, mimicking the larger one at the top of the hill, you know, what better way to streamline the arrival of your children to the College than to have extracurriculars that make them stand out on application, and oh, are also only available at the high school in the same town as the College, a town nonetheless that literally *owns* the College, much like Green Bay and their football team, except this College *is* the town's life, they'd have no economy, no identity without it, well, hey maybe not much as different as Green Bay, but a bigger scale nonetheless, and the kids know the difference between scales, because they practically live on top of a mathematical hybrid of human-reality and nature, for the whole town really is valued exactly as you would imagine the property value of the town would be worth if you did a direct correlation between altitude and cost, when controlling for lake view of course, and it's that slight difference in price which means so much to them, *to them*, when they stand there in their respective lines, one line huff with its own energy, probably annoyed that this intern didn't get the right drink, or that this junior employee doesn't already know the protocol, making it harder to be a mindless manager, when I already put in my ninety-hour weeks, and I should just be able to collect on *fief*, what is life if I'm meant to work past thirty, that would be ridiculous, something for ancient history, human means something more now, something technological, hey perhaps I am of the first generation that will have enough money and technological advancement to live forever, hey yeah, I am probably of the oldest generation that will ever live forever, man I am going to be king for so long, I can't wait to get back to my kingdom, maybe it's time to watch *American Idol* with Melinda and the kids, at least she's finally talking to me now, since I said I like Katharine McPhee more than Taylor Hicks anyway, but that was easy, I wonder what the kids are upto, maybe they'll make a snowman with me this weekend.

A snowman is sitting at the top of a staircase around the other bend, after the shops the road switches to about a seventeen percent gradient and sharply turns, to switchback, now towards where the College sits at the top of the hill, still about a three-quarter mile up, but if you are walking, right after the cheese shop there is a little walk, that takes you past the chocolatier and the french cafe, and some steep stairs that let you bypass the steep turn, there isn't anything to see really anyway, other than some high brick walls, with modern garages built into them, as the houses are about twenty feet up from the road, with bigger properties and some yard, where they connect through the back to the wealthier neighborhoods that surround the College on west and the north, the way the hills roll make it so that behind the houses that are right on the bend are slightly taller and taller houses, so they all can clearly see over the shops towards the lake, and then north of those, to compensate for being obscured by the College, the houses have much bigger properties, with in-ground pools and such, probably closed up and covered with snow, but nonetheless there to keep the active socializing alive outside of the perimeters of the shopping center, from where now the group of professors have just ascended the stairs and are passing by the snowman.

They must be in town just for the final day of the conference considering that they didn't know what bus to take, that or they didn't like the energy of the A bus, maybe I should offer them a ride, it's still a hike up the hill to the college.

"Hey, you all wanna hop in the car? I'm going up the hill!"

T yelled out the window after rolling down next to the group of professors, they were obviously startled by the request, but you could tell the cold had brought a fluster to their face that said they didn't care, *anything warm and getting them there faster would be good*, so they hopped in quickly.

I3

May 28, 2012

Oh what an interesting day *is* today, we are really getting somewhere now!

You see, Raca, chose to actually go to the College this week, rather than stopping for shopping, there was a deal on sweaters at the thrift store last week.

Anyway, when he went there he met again with those *new bosses*, he wasn't very descript and he hasn't gone to them since he first met them.

Again, anyway, they had him come up this week.

He want straight there, so you know he was keen on getting their respect...there is always that need for respect with bosses...he thought...those guys just love it, the more respect the better job they tell you you do, they don't like too much talking, just hard, honest, good work, that is what I do and it is what I can be proud of...

There!

Did you see it, did you see what happened?

He had an emotion!

Maybe because of the emotion that was of the day, *you see*, when he went there, to the College that is, a reporter was also there, it seems it was only a student, as the college had suppressed outside knowledge of the events that had transpired, this at least was clear because you *never* heard anyone talk about it by the chocolatier, *and you know how confectioners love gossip*, he thought to himself once when he was sitting at the french bakery, right before taking a big bite of his chocolate bar and baguette, more crumbs and crumbles falling on his green, button shirt than the day before.

Anyway, when he got to the top of the hill, he did his usual park *thing*, that he would tell himself he was *the professional* at doing, though I don't think there is a person in this town that would pay him to do that, well then I take that back, the *whole* town is paying him to do that, *oof.*

So he walked in the doors and did that thing where he keeps walking briskly, head forward towards the quadrangle, lifts his hand up to the side of his face and *flicks it*, with this determined look in his face, like he's on the case and everybody knows it but he still is *stopping* to say hello, this is what I have gleaned is going on his mind, it must be a composite of movie scenes in his head he thinks his body is telegraphing, but he only *thinks*, he doesn't ever notice that Mabel watches him do this each time with the same repugnant-look on her face, like she can see straight through his brisk walk, his determined eyes, through his pinhole soul to see that gaping hole in his shower crusting over with the disgust of his own *frustration* on the toilet each night, and that that hand might just be the most deadly projectile-launching object walking through that corridor, despite the desert eagle he was allowed and commissioned to have on his hip for the duration of the investigation, his choice on the gun, he said it was the best one in some video game, *and*...that was his reason, and they deputized him with it, he even took a photo pointing it at the camera, but I don't think they ever gave him bullets, don't worry, I know.

So he went through to the quadrangle, after the security office is a hallway on the left, that if you followed it would have you seeing the quadrangle through the large glass windows on the right until you get to the cafeteria where it opens up, like really opens up, at least three levels of seating *arenas*, lifted by thin steel beams, with these weird, star-trek stairs that you barely see, so it looks like the students are floating above each other while they eat their lunch, and there is the one area on the other side where all the faculty launch, I mean eat lunch, like fans in opposing sections of the stadium, and the open-concept kitchen in the center where most of the workers are still employed from out of town, or down the hill, when most of the positions on campus have been given to the students, *so they could have more opportunities to learn*, and so if you went the other way, down the hallway that is, you continue straight towards the quadrangle, with now the glass-panel windows on the left, it makes a spot between the cafeteria and the hallways so there is a grass alcove, surrounded by three walls of glass, I wonder if Raca had a dog, and if they let him bring it to *work*, well they'd let him, if he had one, well I wonder if he'd have it go to the bathroom on that spot of grass in the alcove.

Anyway, opposite the cafeteria from the alcove, is a wall of accolades and the awards of the college and students that have been achieved throughout the years, *but really*...I would puke if we went through that list, it is a list of those achievements that you have to already know what the achievement is to think it's important, and even then *if* you *really* knew what the achievement was, and *how it was achieved*, you might say to yourself, oh, that happened because this person is that person's kid, or this person had access to that which was already this, or something to that effect...Raca said to himself when he passed the wall of Nobel Laureates, Fields Recipients, *Academy* Awards, I think it was the last one that convinced him that he was right, he saw the word academy, and thought to himself *that must mean awards academia gives to itself, so the college comes up with the prizes and tells itself it is prize-worthy*, you know, normally, I would be proud of Raca for having thoughts, but now that they are actually accumulating this is getting rather *frustrating*.

So he walked past the wall, and then was out in the quadrangle, which is really just a term, because this school really does look like a future city in the sky, half of the buildings connected to each other, but at different levels, sporadically, you know to be *trendy*, or to keep the teachers on their toes, or maybe to cause the eager and curious students to eventually wain in their interest of exploring other departments so that they would finally just settle within the collection of staircase-connected-buildings they knew best, or perhaps had gotten permanently lost within, really, sometimes there were more of these students crawling, *not really*, but when there are so many at once in all these different, glass buildings moving from one to the other, the whole place is crawling, like the back of Raca's stove, and none of the students come outside to walk on the paths or sit on the grass, it's odd, maybe because it's too windy sometimes, or because they, in the spirit of Vedici, built the campus to have a perfect lake view from the most amount of windows possible, *seriously*, they flew in a handful of engineers and scholars to figure this out, and they said it was an academic achievement, that's how they got all of the funding.

So the quadrangle does this snaking path thing where it somehow manages to go underneath like ninety-percent of the glass walkways, which now I realize if you walk under you *see* the students and faculty crossing them, not that any one of them are low enough to *really* see anything, but you'd have to think, overtime everyone just got really uncomfortable walking the paths, because they were being thought of as *that person that walked under the walkways*, you know, not because anything was ever done, but because the possibility was there *to look*, and that possibility was too great a destiny that anyone who chose to walk on the path was considered doing so because they *wanted to look*, because why else would they want to be walking down there, *that's where the people that look walk*, and so over time nobody did it anymore and the stigma became even stronger, *I think that is what happened*...you know Raca, *I* think you are actually right this time, but I don't think anyone else has become consciously aware of anything you just stated on this campus before, only you, buddy.

So where is our *investigator* off to now, where is the lead, fella?

"I think I need to go to that *Anderson House* again," Raca muttered to himself while walking off the main path to head towards the building he remembered, the most generic building on campus.

When he got to the building he climbed the stairs to the fourth floor and walked down the glass hallway to the office at the end of the hallway, not the one if you went straight, but right before it, on the left, and in there is a desk, some other professor's, but temporarily occupied by three men and one woman, in suits, that are standing there, well, damn, they closed the door again.

Maybe I can hear instead what Raca is thinking, *in there*, if he is still thinking that is:

"Raca do you know anything new? Hmm, what should I tell them, I could tell them about the techniques I was learning watching *Law & Order: Criminal Intent*, never stop pushing until *they break*, but Goren did say he believes victims need an advocate, I don't know I am conflicted, ah, I wish they didn't cancel that show it was so good, it totally took the series to a different level, oh, they are looking right at me, I forgot anyone was speaking, okay so hmm, anything, new, no not that I can think of."

"Oh shit, no way!"

"Smile, Raca, smile, they are making a joke at your expense, but if you smile, smile, they will be able to see that you are respectful."

Oh look he has already come out, anything new to know, Raca, anything they tell you, nope, he's not thinking about anything, you can see it on his face, he has the slightly upturned lip with his tongue coming-out, yeah there it is, he's going to the chocolatier, they probably just gave him his bonus, he has been eyeing this giant chocolate bear, like really eyeing it, I think *he thinks*, that if he gets it he will be able to control his impulses more directly by reasoning with the bear.

Maybe we should indulge him though, I will stay with him longer, maybe he will think something about what happened when he gets there, he's already down the stairs, by the way, to the way, he took two steps at a time, *on the way down*, and now is skipping through the quadrangle, now all of the students are *looking* at him.

He ran right through the security channel again, and did that damn flick, again, damnit!

Now he is back by his car, pulled out *very fast*, not that he drove fast, but boy did he get out of that spot fast!

He's driving down the hill at acceptable speeds, that's good, he's just turned off of College Ave onto Lake Boulevard, but huh, he's turned right, on MaCarthur, he's going to Copper's it seems, wow, he is still really zipping it, he pulled into the parking lot, and didn't even reverse-park, ran right out, practically leaving it running, the engine hadn't fallen idle before he was on the pavement of the sidewalk, went right towards the glass door, and pulled it open, not even enough time to see what the building looked like, didn't seem like it mattered, he ran towards the first person he saw, which, of course, was a fifteen year old student, who was both startled but instantly amused when they saw Raca come into the school, I don't know if the sudden shock or fear just melted into humor or what, but they had tears building up to meet a grin after they pointed Raca off in some direction he asked for in a mumble only someone who knows what he is talking about already could understand, like when he orders his belgian special at the french bakery, the student darted off to tell their friends of the madman running to, to, oh, the telescope.

It seems they let him get a private viewing, you can tell, because now he is yelling at the student-volunteers that he gets a turn today, not yelling *yelling*, they are students after all, but he sure is frustrated, it seems one of them just pulled out their phone, they already have a picture of him on it from earlier.

It doesn't seem like these student-volunteers are going to help him out, man, they are ribbing him harder than I do, and *that's* saying something, its like they just got the smell of blood, and are now sinking their teeth deep into an *opportunity* to prove just how cool they are in the world diffuse, the one which lives beyond the halls, that *hasn't heard of them yet*, but somehow still holds the same resonate gravity of becoming as anywhere else, that is, so when they go anywhere else they are just waiting for the stars to align so people understand how profound they are, and plus if there aren't any stars there anyway why would they be there, *only the best brah*.

Now some teacher has been alerted to Raca's presence, which seems to be their primary concern despite the small crowd of students that are standing outside the small dome worth more than most other high schools, heckling an *investigator* who is getting paid more than any other investigator has or should be paid, and is now *being assisted*, by this teacher, while he gets his turn operating the telescope, most likely because of the tears welling up in his eyes.

It seems they've really gotten this whole telescope thing down, one of the students made a slideshow that is to synchronize with the movements of the telescope so that when you move to any part of the sky it accesses a hypertext register which pulls information in accordance with where the telescope is placed, like a mouse pointer automatically clicking the spots of the sky to cause the screen to trail behind with the corresponding information, really nice piece of software they made here, but it goes over Raca's head, he is too busy fidgeting the control of the telescope, with each direction prompting him to ask, *is this okay*, because enough times now he has started directioning towards the sun, and still hasn't figured out the whole, object permanence thing, to remember which spots are which in his field of awareness, but can you blame him, the big fella's got such a smile on his face.

He was there about an hour, when the teacher had enough, she really did have patience with him, really, and you can tell he was on his best behavior, he was actually being pleasant after a certain point, it was like something switched in him, when the teacher told him he was finished, he didn't get frustrated, even though he wanted to, he didn't have that air of disdain that always came up when people were taking away things from him, pushing him to the outside, to the fringes, so all he could do would be to watch them through the T.V., to try and be like them, and then when he'd get there they'd laugh at things he'd say, or never know what shows he was referencing, usually incorrectly, because he would get too frustrated with communicating in a way that was pleasant, even though he was trying to be pleasant, he did it just because he knew he had to, and so he would just blurt things out, like, "did you see that new show *Walking Dead*, Shane's going to be a real leader, *huh?*", and people would just say, "*huh?*", not as if they were actually confused, amused really, but they would do it because they didn't know what else to say, or what else to do with Raca, he frustrated his way through everything, either making people angry to get himself in the process angier, or they would just laugh, it was their power over him, they thought, to laugh, rather than figure out where it all went wrong, man, I have been trying to figure it out for a long time now, really have, and I just think, I think something switched, really, you could see it in his face, she told him he was done, and his face whipped towards her at first, like a child getting an extra piece of cake taken away, but then that smile bubbled back through, he looked at her like he must have looked at someone else in his past, and he realized what she did for him, how much she changed things for him in that moment, that moment he had all the power in the world and still none of it could conquer the difficulty of his own body, yet she came in, knowing exactly what needed to be done, and helped him, *you know Goren was right*, he said to himself, and walked proudly to his car, having, perhaps, finally seen the stars he was never able to see, on the top of one of the most prosperous towns at the most prestigious high school in this universe, and maybe several other.

Except, this stupid doofus, and I will use stupid here, because there are moments, and then *there are moments*, and this was such a moment, so like I was saying, before I got all caught up in it, he was leaving to his car, when this kid from the College caught back up with him, some gawky kid that must have caught wind of Raca's presence when everyone had seen him skipping, and he came right up to Raca, first looking at his phone like he was confirming something, and then flipped it around to use the camera, to take video, like all these kids had started doing, capturing everything and sending it to each other, feeling emboldened, thinking the possession of the curation of their media will lead to more power for themselves, as if the power results in what they can curriculate, curriculate all you want, but if you don't know what you are building, how can you really say you have something to circulate, anyway, he starts filming and yelling at Raca, like he is trying to instigate him or something, and Raca was shook, really, he thought his day was over, he was ready to reflect on that moment for the rest of his life, and this kid started mocking Raca, making fun of his body, his tears, telling him that he was the lead investigator in a witch hunt, and that he was just a pig, and asked him if he had anything to say.

Raca didn't say anything, *of course not*, but he still hasn't, he came right home, skipped his soaps, the television kind, *obviously*, and went right to sleep.

14

June 4th,

three nights before the trial:

"...it is nice to meet you."

"Nice to meet you as well, you said your name is Raca?"

"That's right!"

"So how can I help you today, Raca?"

"Well, I wanted to ask you about Professor Cinotau, it is my understanding that you've known each other for quite some time, perhaps longer than anyone else I have interviewed?"

"I am not sure if I can answer that for you Raca, but yes I have known Professor Cinotau for quite some time."

"Would you be willing to answer some character questions, you know so we could get an understanding of temperament?"

"Yes, certainly."

"Would you say Professor Cinotau was a friendly person?"

"Without a doubt, Professor Cinotau was always cordial towards me, and towards my family.

When my oldest was applying for schools, Professor Cinotau actually helped advise decisions and wrote a recommendation letter."

"What did the letter say?"

"Well, I didn't read it. It was sent off to the school."

"You didn't read it? Probably not a good idea to be sending off applications without proofreading them, that's why I didn't go to college...*mistakes*."

"You didn't go to college?

And you became a lead investigator, well you were still able to find some success then, that's good."

"That is *nice* of you to say.

Okay, next question.

Did you ever witness Professor Cinotau getting angry or frustrated towards anyone?"

"Well, I have to think about that.

I don't think so, no I don't, it's just that sometimes I felt aggression but I wasn't sure."

"Like you were being *incited*!"

"No, I wouldn't call it that, it was more, nevermind, it's just, do you ever get that feeling that someone is watching all the decisions you make, and saying things about you but you don't ever know?"

"No I don't think that has ever happened to me."

"Well, nevermind then."

"Okay, next question.

Had you ever seen Professor Cinotau get overly emotional?"

"I am not sure I have seen that happen, well, actually I take that back, just the other day..."

"...the other day?"

"Well, yeah, there was some reporter that was talking to Professor Cinotau and I did see a lot of emotional expression, it looked like it had gotten very heated."

"Did the reporter look like a doofus?!"

"Excuse me?"

"Nevermind.

So you have seen Professor Cinotau upset, so what, everyone gets upset.

Next question."

"Okay."

"*Okay.*"

"Are you going to ask it?"

"You bet!"

"Okay."

"*Next question*, do you ever hear Professor Cinotau espouse political views."

"Well, I might have, I mean hasn't everyone?"

"So yes, I am writing *yes*.

Professor Cinotau has espoused radical political views."

"That's not what I said."

"*Is it?*"

"I am sorry, did I do something to offend you?"

"No you have been nice...very *nice*."

"Well, I would like to state that I am not *sure* if Professor Cinotau has espoused *radical* political views."

"So it is possible?"

"I guess you could say that."

"Thank you.

Next question.

Did you ever see any students going off campus with Professor Cinotau?"

"Do you mean, did Professor Cinotau meet with the students privately?"

"Yes."

"No, not that I know of, as far as I know Professor Cinotau did not."

"Did you have any disagreeances with Professor Cinotau?"

"Well, throughout the years we had several, there were plenty of things for us to disagree about, you know."

"Any about theories?"

"Oh, no, none about theories or anything like that...well, may I ask what you mean when you say *theories*."

"*Theories.*

That is what they *make* at the College.

Professor Cinotau had been working on some theories that had incited the students causing them to revolt so we are building a case to investigate whether or not these theories are real, or that it is credible Professor Cinotau would create these theories."

"Well, did you interview the students or review the classroom material?"

"The parents don't consent to the students being interviewed."

"Aren't they adults?"

"*I am asking the questions here.*"

"I am sorry.

I just mean to say I was unaware that the students could *not* be questioned."

"As far as I know the school or *that town* doesn't allow it, but I haven't been asked to ask them any questions, I am asking *you* the questions."

"Hey I got it, no need to be frustrated."

"I am not frustrated.

We already looked through the classroom material, we couldn't find anything that told the students to *revolt*, no plans or manifestos."

"I didn't think that was how those things happen."

"Don't take that tone with me, I am the *investigator*."

"Hey listen guy, I am not going to spend my Monday afternoon being harassed."

"Sir, could you please sit back down, I am not done asking the questions."

"Fine, but you need to calm yourself."

"I will."

"Okay."

"*Okay.*"

15

Eighth Class

"So, James, any luck in finding out any information about Professor Cinotau?" Professor Dillinger asked for the first time, since, you know, James *said* he would look for information.

"Well, actually, it has proved quite difficult," James said before tufting his hair.

"Have you attempted the library, yet?" Professor Dillinger replied looking not at James, but the other three students.

"Well, of course, I tried that after the internet." James said.

"And?"

"Well, there is *nothing* on the internet."

"Right," Professor Dillinger said now looking out the window at the clouds, "Professor Cinotau was at this school when the internet was just starting to taking root in this society."

Mallory yawned.

"Well, there is nothing at the library, so now I don't know what to do," James said.

"*There is* plenty at the library," Professor Dillinger said incredulously, to no one's adoration but his own.

"Well, what I mean, is that there are no books listed under the name Cinotau, and I thought that would be enough to go off of, but I am not sure," James said looking to the Professor who, now, was finally making eye contact.

"Huh, no books...that's strange," Professor Dillinger said, still holding the eye contact, "Maybe you should try asking around to see what people remember?"

16

10:41 am - Sunday

"Hey, thanks for the ride!" said the taller of the three as they got in the car.

The tallest electing to sit up front, probably for the leg room, she's most likely junior faculty at some school in the midwest, judging by her clothes and genial attitude, the stamp-mark statement, nonetheless always true, there is something about the similarity, I mean you have to imagine that the same people who called the midwest the fly-over states are the same ones who said just how hokey they are, but it's more than just a difference of attitude, there is something coded-in, it's not just oh she's nice, unless you yourself are nice and you value that word, but instead it's oh she's not offensive, or more accurately, *offensible*, you can go and say what you want, they aren't like they are in other parts of the country, they know manners there, when you walk in and want immediate service because you just got off the highway and this is the only diner about ten miles from anywhere, and you are still more worried about making time to the City than you are about the kids losing their way to the bathroom, that you'd then have to tell the guys at work you didn't get to go jet skiing on the great lake because little bart got kidnapped, no, not in the midwest, they are nice, there is something occupational in that, something that just keeps you that way, nice, nice, not able to do much more than that, and it let alone being known for a whole entire area of the country, imagine what you'd think of each other, man who would be the nicest on the block, certainly not Frank, that's for sure, *he is too nice*, nobody would think he was actually nice, he's just nice because it's easy for him to be nice, he almost has to be nice, it would be rude if he wasn't, he knows we all share the water utility on the block and both his fountain and swimming pool get completely drained and filled for cleaning every two years, instead of five, because *the exotic flowers' pollen scums the bottom of the jet mechanism in a way that can only be cleaned when its drained*, and now everybody on the block has to have a heart-attack every other year when they see their bill in July, man it's the summer, let people have their money for the vacations they don't get to have, that you keep telling them about, so you can seem nice when you are walking with your kids, who look at everyone else as if they're citizens of the fiefdom, that one day dad might somehow own the whole block.

In the back get in two people who might actually be the exact same height, completely different people, but somehow ended up the same exact height, same proportions, really, it's odd to see them next to each other, they look nothing alike, but somehow life found them at a certain disposition that seemed to informed them to the same style of dress, the same way of sitting, and raising your hand to above your ear when you are responding to a joke, as if at that height you need to hear just a little better than any others before responding, really, they both keep doing it, at intervals, maybe their subconscious is aware, because I am aware, you know like when people are walking in complete unison, stride for stride like the birds, and then someone says something and they all scatter in every direction, legs kicking like they don't know which way is the ground because they keep trying to match something that was never real in the first place, now they are both looking at me look at them in the mirror, I wonder if they have the same thoughts.

"So you've been to every day of the conference this year?", asked the one sitting behind T, "This is our first year here, we didn't know how many activities there were each day, we would have come in sooner," she dipped her head a little towards the center so her eyes could meet T in the mirror.

They were a deep blue, contrasting the dark, tight dreads that hung by her cheeks, some wrinkles folded around her eyes when she finished her question due to a big smile she gave, so T would know they weren't bummed by the news.

"No, no I just come in for the end of the conference as well," T said looking back through the mirror and giving a smile.

The car was starting to fog up a little from the shift in temperature and the extra bodies emitting radiating heat from their walk through the thick snow, the sidewalks were barely shoveled, and since the sun had come out the snow was heavy and wet, T could smell a mix between the pine that sometimes captures itself in the snow, probably a build-up in the clouds and water from the forest grove that gets swept in before the storm and settles in the snow to be lifted up when it melts, that bright white snow, makes the air feel moist and helps the light from the sun to bake those that are wearing insulting jackets, big ones much better suited for the midwest, now in a car all too warm, causing the coat's recalcitrant nature to being fastened by seat belts with comfort to cause them to come off for the duration of the short car ride, so mixed with the pine is the fresh body odor settling in from the underarms, as T opens the window just a little bit, which causes a small stream of air to pass through by the side air bag, straight through to the hatch, where now the latch is jettisoned open, and quickly closed, click.

"Oh Marguerite, tell, T about the nightmare...*or uh*...dream you had last night," the taller one, I think her name is Maggie, Maggie said to Marguerite, right Marguerite, that's it, "T, I think you'd find this interesting."

She turned towards T and gave a big grin.

She had nice teeth to match her nice face.

"I don't know about just telling everybody as if it's some news, you might give people the wrong idea," said Henry, or Herbert, or something with an 'H'.

"Don't listen to Hermes, T, he's just a worrywort it seems, we met him down by the station after we all got off on the wrong bus," T, looked in the mirror at Hermes, who was now looking at Marguerite with a similar toothy grin as Maggie, T was unsure of whether or to believe what was being said, but nonetheless laughed along with the group.

They were now passing by a large brick building, large, both the building and the bricks, one of those temple looking structures, it is called *Dan Copper's High Performance School for the Gifted*, a place that earns more money in donations than a telethon, and has some sub-disciplines, *you know ones for the kids to take so they can figure out what kind of stuff they like*, that universities haven't even heard of before.

There are about a handful of lists for first achievements that they share with notable names and some nations, they may have invented a new type of recycling program, or perhaps recycling itself, I think the kids are all demigods that float on clouds and have those mystical portal table things that allow them to see as if they are flying in a cloud over the ground somewhere else, but it's the inside of Vedici High and they are causing the lab equipment to break like it usually does, or tripping kids in the hallway, or giving them acne or something, or making that one teacher who could make a difference always late so that when the class starts they already know they aren't being given access to the *real* world but someone else who has been rejected so even though there are so many similarities to you and students, in what you care about and want to do, and you should be the perfect teacher, they never see you more than their friend and your ideas as pathways to just believing in the things you are trying to warn them about, how you stand like an inspiration for decadence, but they don't even know what that word means, that it ultimately means downfall, and that this earth wasn't made for us to all fall down, and those that *really do and get up*, and talk about it, didn't have to fall down *down here*, where falling means sinking, and sinking means sunken, for years and years, not for that one weekend hiking, or that trip to the tree, no, but seeing the whole world cave in and never being able to believe that the reality you knew when you were younger was real, not even being able to remember it, what it meant to have hope, what there is even to hope for, for what I even am, any...any of them could be just messing with each other, I am not really sure, Hermes, that's his name, got to remember that.

"Okay, so this is really the weirdest dream, so you really need to listen the whole way there, if you want to get the effect," the car fell silent, as T oscillated between looking: at the road about a quarter mile until the beginning of College Road, and then it is a about another half mile through the big loop that climbs the campus to get to the *Affinity Parking Lot*, I think they just named it that, I don't know, but I got to listen; to Marguerite, "okay, so, I was about thirteen when this first happened, *to me really that is*, when I was thirteen I had gone to the beach with my family, it was up by the cape, we had hiked for the day to find someplace private so we could have a picnic without the seagulls that crowd the more frequently used spots, so about noon we came upon the perfect spot, crescent-shaped shoreline with light, lapping waves, and had one of those alcoves, *Beaches* kind of feel to it you know.."

"...I think you mean *The Beach*," said Hermes, to a quick jab from Marquirite, then she pinched him right under the lapel, and he gave her a smirk, "hey, I just want to make sure you get it right!"

"...okay so, at *the beach*, when I am thirteen, and I've taken myself about fifty feet away from my parents, we had finished lunch, or I had for the most part, because they were eating those weird after-dinner cheese spreads, or at least they always liked having it after dinner, and it was the garlic one, so it was just no thank you, not ending with that at the beach to bake in my teeth, thank goodness my dad drove a Jeep, otherwise I would never go on those trips, well, anyway, this one was different, so I was about fifty feet away, and I noticed that the water from the ocean was trailing over the sand and not receding in one spot, it made a light stream, but you know how the sand is, it kind of looked like the grand canyon, and I got real excited because it looked just like it and I remember learning in geography that year that the Pueblo people would take pilgrimages to the grand canyon, and I had been collecting those really nice sticks that wash up on the beach, the driftwood ones, and the one I had picked up had this wedge at the top of it so I put this really pretty seashell, not to make a weapon, it was more like a sceptre, more feminine, and so when I saw the stream I thought it looked like the grand canyon and that my stick was a prayer stick, so I ran over to it, and started jumping and dancing, and saying prayers to the stream, like stream you are mighty you are strong you can reach the farthest destinations, and each successive lap of a wave would come in and push the stream farther and farther, and I think I was dancing around it for about thirty minutes, when finally the sand just caved in, it completely sunk, in one spot, like a small pit or well, and I sat and watched it, and the water kept flowing to just sink, submerge serenely, down this well, or well, whatever it was, I was so enamored by it I put down the prayer stick, standing-up in the ground about four inches back from it, and put it deep in the ground until it was just about two inches tall with the shell about an inch above that, and I built a three-quarters circle around both of them, with the well in the center, I think I used the shadow from the prayer stick, which was about eleven on a clock or whatever, so it went out around the back of the prayer stick and to the sides of the stream, but not all the way because I didn't want to cause it to cave in at an earlier point, and because of that I decided not to build a castle, which was what my plan initially was going to be, and right when I was about to doubt my change of mind, the sun, which had started to set, now sat directly opposed to the seashell, or at least I noticed it right then, so that the light hit the well and the seashell was reflected in the water, while the shadow from the prayer stick was now exactly at noon, and it stretched the long way to the wall of the alcove, and so I got up and I ran, right towards where it landed, and I couldn't believe..."

"...We're here." Hermes said as T had just pulled into spot *2B*, then quickly got out of the car, the two women followed, laughing while T sat still, unsure of what to do, I don't have time to think about it, got to just go follow them, T got out of the car to stretch, the whole parking lot was pristine, not just because it was pristine, I mean it was *pristine,* but because it sat at the top of the entire town, and now the sun was firmly shining on its wet black-tops, with the thick-yellow lines that have the reflective material laced into the paint, so that nobody will ever get wrong which spot is which, and, and T, grabbed the bag which had been still sitting on the grey, leather chair, now saturated by the runoff of sweat and melted snow that was trapped between the insulated jacket, and the heated-leather, and the flap was open, damn, man, the moisture was condensating or whatever, my papers have been cooked liked broccoli, now all my pages are running clean, and that's the benefit of using fountain pen ink, isn't it T, always say you'll never spill anything, no never would, not you T, how could it ever get ruined, this is how it gets ruined, man, I don't know if I can read this, and I could barely read it when it was dry, I don't know how they are going to let me present with this I don't have anything, man.

"Hey T, are you coming?" Marguerite was still standing on the curb of the parking lot, while Hermes and Maggie had interlocked arms and were faux-skipping towards the main entrance of the college, it was quite a sight to see, but I don't really have time to explain, man, I'm thinking about what it is I am going to have to say, to *have* to say.

"Yes, I am on my way, my apologies, was just making sure I had all my stuff!" T, said with an odd-enthusiasm, but it went unnoticed by Marguerite who was still holding up the levity of the other two.

The walk up to the main entrance had a rhombic shape, with rows of planted trees, small trees on raised stone-encased dirt plots, that ran parallel to the borders of the walk, there were about six trees on either side, and they got closer and closer together as you got towards the entrance, which had a big arched window over the steel and glass double doors, you could see straight into the building through to the quadrangle on the otherside, even though it was about forty feet away, from the doors, which were now being sung open by Hermes and Maggie, opening to a large foyer, that could also be seen from outside, the whole facade was glass, really, but the way it was tinted caused the arched windows and the doors to seem like a separate aspect, well, you could see the foyer which was designed to have an inclusive environment, essentially all of the schools most influential administrative positions had their offices clustered in little cubby-divisions, like the *Hollywood Squares* show, so that when you entered the school you were in what was *actually the backbone to the school*, and this was the main entrance, there was no other way to enter, you had to come through this gate, and gate quite literally, you know, inclusive entrance, but each office has bullet-proof glass and panic buttons, and the ground level administrative offices where you walk through are the security and campus safety offices, but nonetheless, you see them there everyday, all the administrators, making the school what it is, like ants on display, *so the students can never argue about what it is, and who it is, that put their effort into making this place the way it is*, their words not mine, at least that's what they were telling everyone when they passed the budget to build themselves the new campus, it is actually quite interesting the history of the whole campus, but I've got to get through to where everyone else is now or I'll miss my opportunity, I just know it, today is going to be a big day.

I7

June 5th, 2012

...today must have been a good day...well the whole week has started good, for Raca, that is, he has gotten to *actually* investigate, well interrogate, but nonetheless, he has been given *responsibility*, he knows how important it is so he was making sure that he had all of his papers properly stacked on his table, which isn't hard considering at this point there are now *three*, and he was on-time to the College each day this week.

They've had him do two interviews already, well *one*, but he hasn't gotten back yet, from the second, but now he was really feeling like a true investigator, he felt nervous at first, you know, whether or not he would go *too hard* on the witnesses, but he knew that he had to get good testimony because they said they would be using these as the *main* evidence, I don't understand it, but nonetheless, on his first day, he was surprised, not because *she was a woman*, just because he realized he didn't prepare any techniques for women, and wasn't sure if the same strategy was used, because sometimes things were different, he knew that, he wanted to be fair to everyone.

"Her name was Margaret." He wrote down when he got back. "She is a close friend of Professor Cinotau. She knew about the events that *transpired*. It is possible she knows more than she stated. She said Professor Cinotau wasn't there when *it* happened."

He read over it about fifty times, making sure every letter would be legible in case he looked at it next week and his handwriting was already different, because he didn't write much, his hands would always get too stiff, and then he would forget the way he was supposed to make certain letters, so he would always be throwing his hand back quickly to correct letters *that he could read* but didn't have a *serif* or whatever lithographic character he mistakenly took the teacher to be informing him was the essence of the lesson, so that he would be constantly correcting himself to the point that he'd have to take a break because his hand hurt, he would ice it and get frustrated because now his homework would take twice as long and he wouldn't be allowed to watch T.V. until it was finished, so then he would get back to his homework after icing, because his 'm'am' would at least let him eat a snack when he iced his hand, because if he didn't he would just push right through the pain to get on to T.V. because the *X-files* was on and he just loved how Skinner would dig into Mulder for not following protocol, and Skully would say aliens weren't real, *not* because he didn't believe in those things, he very much believed in those things, or at least he used to...his memory would get foggy when he thought about it, so he likes the more true crime shows these days...but his hand would be hurting so much that he wouldn't be sure what he felt and he just knew that he sympathized with Mulder in those moments, and Mulder was his favorite character, he loved that one line...*wait*...so, anyway, he would remember to ice, and have his pudding-cup, and then he would also have to half some walnuts, both for the exercise to warm his hand back up, but also because he needed to eat protein, he knew from watching television, to get muscles, and also he learned on the morning news that nuts are good for you, so he ate a lot of walnuts, *to lose weight*, and when he would return back to his homework, he'd usually have to start over because he could never read what he wrote, or remember what he was working on to figure it out, that he would just start over, but then usually would be competing both with the sounds in his head that were what he could remember from the first time, and what he just generally knew as his memory, but it would start getting louder and louder, not that it was telling him to do things, but it would suggest certain ways he should believe in *himself*, that he started to let the noise be louder than his focus on what he...where was *I*, oh my god, where have I been...and the noise would take over...I have been stuck like *this*, *this*, for so long....what he could process has its own focus...today must have been a good day...today must have been a good day...well the whole week has started good, for Raca, that is, he has gotten to *actually* investigate, well interrogate, but nonetheless, he has been given *responsibility*, he knows how important it is so he was making sure that he had all of his papers properly stacked on his table, which isn't hard considering at this point there are now *four*, and he was on-time to the College each day this week.

They've had him do three interviews already, well *two*, but he hasn't gotten back yet, from the third, but now he was really feeling like a true investigator, he felt nervous at first, you know, whether or not we would go *too hard*, on the witnesses, but he knew that he had to get good testimony because they said they would be using these as the *main* evidence, I don't understand it, but nonetheless, on his third day, he was surprised, not because *she was a woman*, just because he realized he didn't prepare any techniques for women, and wasn't sure if the same strategy was used, because sometimes things were different, he knew that, he wanted to be fair to everyone.

"Her name is Melissa." He wrote. "She is a close friend of mine. She knows about motives and *conspiracy*. She definitely knows about much more. She thinks Professor Cinotau *is* innocent."

He read over it about fifty times, making sure every letter would be legible in case he looked at it next week and his handwriting was already different, because he didn't write much, his hands would always get too stiff, and then he would forget the way he was supposed to make certain letters, so he quickly threw his hand back to correct the letters so that *he could read it.*

Then he put the papers back into the manila folder, and slid it into a small crevice in the wall behind the stairs, *hah*, not a bad spot after all, and he went upstairs, huh, that's early, *oh my*, he's looking in the mirror...he's smiling!

...And just as quickly, he's dashing out the front door, he took his stairs down two steps at a time, to great effect, shaking his right-triangular home, as he ran right through the blinding abyss to reach the door without losing his balance, he had that lip and tongue thing going on again, and I'm pretty sure he thought about doing the flick.

We are driving down the street, now, that I can see it, I have to say, it's actually not that bad, the neighborhood that is, the street still isn't filled, the rain had been making the potholes blend in with the road, the grey skies that had been accumulating since the weekend made the matter all the worse, so, despite his relative mood, there was no preventing this...*splasssh...popopopop...splasssh...popopopop*...ahh, I hate that, how can you enjoy going anywhere with this every which way outside your home, anyway, Raca doesn't seem to mind, there is somewhere else he is supposed to be *in his mind*, and as far as I can tell his mind is *already there* and his body is following after to meet him.

His house makes a lot more sense when you see it from the outside, it seems like *at some point*, someone intended for the property to be a high-yield chicken plot, not for slaughter, *think earlier*, you know when everyone had to get their own eggs each morning, rather than pay someone to *harvest* meat, and whatnot, and they respected their relationship with the chickens, well, somebody in the neighborhood must have thought it would be helpful, or *profitable*, to have a yard where a lot of chickens could be housed, *comfortably*, and produce several eggs for the neighborhood.

You could imagine Raca's house, its right-triangular prism shape, in the corner of its square-plot, so that the house had its roof, which was sloped and thatched, to hold protection from the elements over the perimeter of the house, so that at the far end to about the T.V. was space for coops to be securely built up against the frame of the house, and from the T.V. to staircase area you could see pits, they have since been filled, but at one time held support beams so that the thatched roof could be lifted and extend to the other end of the plot, allowing space for even more coops to be installed, and then most of the space *is* the yard, so that the chickens can be free-ranged, and there could be *a lot* of them, I like to imagine, a sedentary ancestor of Raca's once had the home, and would sit in the house, it looking probably just the same as the day it was built except for the modern appliances, sitting at his table, eating walnuts, while thirty or some chickens are running around his plot, fifteen more climbing the roof, squawking all day, while he has that same half-turned smile on his face that Raca has right now.

We took the freeway, which he usually doesn't take, not because he is a bad driver, he gets frustrated with how other people drive, driving was something he had always been very good at, not in *that aggressive way* people mean when they like to tell other people they are good, or the defensive *way* other people claim *they* drive, usually to say in response to say that their *good* is better, he, however, was extremely polite and courteous, *the helping grandma cross the street equivalent of a driver on the road*, he would get frustrated because of how people treated *other* people on the road, he didn't like the loss of control, of not being able to say something or do anything, not that he would have said or done anything if something similar happened on the sidewalk, those things he never noticed, usually when he picked his head up to look around when walking in public, it was to confirm whatever he, *resolutely*, was thinking, or just had become thinking because the thought had compelled him in the first place, but on the road he felt relaxed in the chair, able to look at everyone without them *really* looking at him, it felt just like television to him, so there he is, driving in the middle lane, after making sure to first wait for the on-ramp dividing line to *break*, before crossing, and waited a tenth of a mile before merging into the middle lane.

The road is completely empty, unusual for this time of the day, but it could just be one of those *of the moment* things, where when you pull on, you've just gotten on after a whole fleet of cars that had been congregating together have passed through the area so that there's a delay until those that weren't caught in its gravity have caught up, he stays on it for two miles, he is heading towards his local shopping center, his town is separated by a few highways, so if he wants to go shopping he usually plans it accordingly to which stores are in which area and then separates it for different days, which is why he thinks Vedici is such a great town, not because of anything *they say about it*, because they do say a lot, but because all of the shops are near each other and in such a way it's easy for anyone to come in and feel like they are a customer.

Not that he went shopping frequently, but it would be difficult in his town to go from store to store all at once and still make it home in time for the early-afternoon programming, his favorite time of the television schedule, he loved to watch *Days of our Lives*, recently on the show most of the cast had confronted Stefano, who is this mega-villain, he's *really* evil, he was this big boss of a crime organization, and caused political terrorism, and had a business that stole from others *their business*, but at the same time he was a loving, family man, I nev...I mean Raca, didn't know whether to hate him or love him, either way he drew *a lot* of emotion, cheeks moving, ears wiggling, his nose *may* have wrinkled, and I think his shoulders flexed a little bit, Raca that is, Stefano has that type of charm that makes you question everything you've ever known, but at the same time he's double-crossing you so you can never trust him even though you are loving him, it's too much, well, anyway, the rest of the characters thought so too, not that the *character* was too much, that would be a weird perspective for a character in a story to think, but that Stefano was too much, had done too much, finally crossed enough lines, and everyone went to confront Stefano, and it was big and emotional, and then, and then, someone shot Stefano...*I was there*, I was there when Stefano was shot and killed...anyway, and now Roman, this impartial officer is questioning everyone to figure out who assassinated Stefano.

Wherever we are going must be good, if Raca is missing this right now, I kind of wish he would go home, but nonetheless, he's sailed the freeway.

18

June 3rd,

four nights before the trial:

"Hi, it is nice to meet you, your name is Margaret?"

"Marguerite!"

"Yes, okay, so miss, may I ask you some questions."

"That's why I am here!"

"Are you familiar with Professor Cinotau?"

"Yes, we are long friends we go back to the beginning."

"You are a sister?"

"Well...no I am not."

"So you should be able to tell me about the young Professor Cinotau?"

"Sure, why not?"

"Okay great! I appreciate your assistance, you are being very helpful today."

"*Okay.*"

"What was that?"

"Nothing."

"So first, tell me about yourself, where you grew up, what kind of stuff do you like to do...I mean what job do you have?"

"Well, *okay*, I grew up on the coast, I have been in school since I was little, one way or another, and have been a visiting professor at Hillbrandt for the last semester."

"So you were on campus when the events took place?"

"Actually I was, Professor Cinotau also taught on Wednesdays.

So I should have been having my class, *Gateways: Where Metaphor meets Narrative*, that is, around the same time that things transpired."

"Were you able to witness any of the events?"

"I may have."

"You may?

Well what happened?"

"That's not what you asked."

"Well I am asking now, what happened?"

"I don't know if I want to say."

"It was that bad, huh? Did they bring out a gully-teen?"

"A what...oh no...it was nothing, *nothing*, like that, are you seriously asking that question?"

"They didn't tell me much."

"Clearly."

"So you could give an account then, *in your words*."

"Yes, I *could*."

"Ugh!"

"You know you could do a better job of asking questions and researching the case."

"That's not up to me."

"Who is it up to then?"

"My *bosses*."

"Well they aren't doing a good job of *being your bosses*."

"That is not correct to say!

They do a very good job.

You need to have some more respect for the authority around here, they are *your employer too*, after all."

"Do you do everything your bosses tell you?"

"Well, yes, that is what being an employee means, do *you* do everything that the Dean tells you?"

"No, not at all, actually."

"Then you must be a pretty bad teacher."

"Actually, I am not, my students *love me*."

"I am sure they do, and you know *what*, I am sure that soon enough they are going to *love* you so much that they are going to revolt against the Dean for you, if you aren't careful."

"Hey that's not true, none of these students have it in them for a real revolution."

"What...what now?"

"They don't care enough, you can already see it, they all feel too much pace and speed in everything they are doing, which is great for *when you want to revolt*, but not when you want an actual, *real* revolution, they don't allow time to find their niche and settle, to let the space take over their character of being, so they are able to become one with the narrative and environment of their space, they are usually just hopping from space to space, role to role, wanting to be this and that so they are proficient at everything, but they really don't learn a single thing the way you are supposed to, *really*, I have students that still come to class asking for assistance with their *outfits* sometimes, this one girl didn't know how to braid her own hair and she had forgotten to get her mom to do it that weekend, and her roommate had to go to practice early in the morning, and *then*, I have another student ask me how many of the homework assignments does he have to turn in to get a B, for a class that *doesn't even have at-home assignments*, everything is about *willing* classroom participation, and I don't know, he may have been messing with me, they may all just be messing with us, but these students *are seriously* different than the kids at the school I was teaching at before this, and I am sure it will only catch-up, they say Hillbrandt is the flower of the whole world of schooling, whatever happens here is liable to fly off the hill and end up pollinating somewhere else, and it usually does, and these kids know it too, that's what really gets me, actually, they know it, they know they are too good for everyone else, that they get more than everyone else, that they will see a completely different world than everyone else, but they are still kids, nonetheless, you are giving kids all these opportunities that should be given to *teachers*, let alone kids fresh out of high school being told they can run the summer chemlab program so they can get experience, while millions in funding is going to allow them to blunder, how does that *really* teach them about the *real* world, they are just being taught that they can take money from other people, burn it to the ground, and get away with it!"

"I'm sorry I may not have been following all that...but you said that Professor Cinotau's students were burning money outside the class?"

"No."

"Then do you mind telling me *what did* happen?"

"Fine.

All I saw were a few students that seemed very excited running from the building, you knew something was up because they were on the ground, you know, on the path, not in the glass walkways, so it looked like they were trying to *leave* campus, which students don't really do in that fashion, *but*, at the same time there were the few students running excited, and a whole rest of them running after, like they were chasing the students."

"Perhaps to help, because Professor Cinotau had poisoned their minds?

Maybe they were running after them with the antidote."

"I don't think so."

"Then what did you say happened, in your words."

"Well, maybe there were a few students who had gotten emotionful, or excited, and the other students instigated them, and it got out of hand or something, I don't know, I just don't think Professor Cinotau had anything to do with it."

"Why is that?"

"I didn't *see* Professor Cinotau running with the students, or really, after that, *at all.*"

I9

Ninth Class

"So, James.

Anything new?" Professor Dillinger asked reluctantly.

"Well, yes!" James said, remembering he had something to say, "Yes, there is any..something new!"

"Well...what is it?" asked Mallory, straining her neck enough so that she could look at her seatmate talk.

"Well, so get this, I was downtown with a few of my buddies and we were going to the shops, because sometimes we like to think it is funny if we pretend to be adults, you know go shopping and stuff, and so we went to the chocolatier, and my one friend, John, he's talking about how he's got this assignment that he had to do which made him go to the library and look up *the canon*...so then I'm like what...that's wild I had to go look up something that starts with a "c" as well, and so I am telling him about it, and the chocolatier comes out from behind the counter, and you know that guy he never moves, not like that fish market owner, and he says, 'Cinotau? I have heard that name before, some guy was in here long ago mumbling about this and that and he said something about Cinotau and the student newspaper...so before he finished speaking I ran out of the place and right to the library so that I wouldn't forget..." James said looking at Professor Dillinger.

"And...then?" Mallory said, you could tell her neck hurt.

"Well, and then I ran to the library...well you know to the bus, the A was going by, it wasn't there when I ran out but then I saw it at the bend of the hill and raced to the stairs so I could beat it and get on at the next stop, at the top of the stairs...I probably didn't need to run and should have asked John to come but he was talking to the chocolatier about some bear or something...first they were talking about something about some jail that had to let a bank go free or something...and then something about a market...and then they were talking about bears...yeah some chocolate bear...it was weird so I left...I mean I had to go the library." James said tufting his hair twice while he spoke.

"*Uh huh?*" Mallory yapped, she may have tried saying something, but her larynx looks slightly compressed.

"Well, so I find out that the student newspaper had records going all the way back to 1963, something about the press being by committee or something before that...and I didn't really know what year to look, so I figured probably no better place to start than to look at the beginning...and so I went through every file...*really*, Professor every file," James said to the, again, incredulous Professor Dillinger, "and I was skimming through them at first and they were mostly just articles at the beginning about different ways of getting dressed or talking...and socializing and such...then it was more about what things people talk about and how they can talk to each other about those things with *relevance*...and then they were talking about a lot of the *relevant* issues and what some of the well-dressed and well-spoken people were thinking and talking about them...and then it was just about the well-dressed and well-spoken people talking about things...then they weren't talking about things anymore...and then they weren't that well-dressed or well-spoken...but there was a lot more stuff that was *relevant*, apparently, so they started talking about different ways of addressing or talking about the *relevant things*...so that you could be social and stuff...they almost started advocating for it...and then they were advocating for a lot of things...and all these people who looked just like the well-dressed and well-spoken people came back but they weren't talking about the things with *relevance* but were saying what *is relevant*...until I didn't know what was going on anymore...and that's when I saw it."

"Saw what?" Mallory muttered from the fold of her elbow, her head now resting on the desk.

"'*End of Semester: A professor was investigated by the administration via an independent judicial agent leading to their expulsion from record.*'"

20

11:42 am - Sunday

When they had walked through the doors, T and Marguerite, Hermes and Maggie, that is, they were first encountered by a group of undergraduates, who had volunteered for the day and were set up at a small table at the entrance, there were only a few remaining name-badges on the table it seemed, and at first T was nervous, because the two students there, Peter and Mabel, their name-badges said, being students weren't in a meaningful way connected to any of the faculty, so T quickly planned to reference some project that had required assistance, to suggest that T was the one being called, but without saying those words of course, or that anyone even needed to be called, so no lies were really spoken, but rather now that wasn't possible, because Peter and Mabel, while being naive to the world around them, were well-equipped towards the mechanism of the terminus, and with great delicacy were checking identification and lists, equipped with the great power to decide whether or not this narrative would go on, and there T stood less sure of what to say, or what to do, and as they walked up to the table Maggie looked right at Mabel, and said T was here a few days before, had to go to another conference yesterday, very tired, and was walking with them from the bus when T's bag fell to the ground, to tumble open over the snow, *because of the hills in this town*, and all of T's work was ruined or lost, along with the name-badge, and that T needed access to an office right now to rearticulate some of the notes as they were needing to present later today, so if they could please help us that would be greatly appreciated, we are all a little flustered, she said, to great effect, you could tell the students cared.

So here T sits, this just happening eleven minutes earlier, now sitting in the office of a distinguished professor of the College, Professor Gershom was it, with a small personal library sitting to the left, a desk with notebooks filled with writing, and some with some space in them, man, what can I do with this, my plan was to get *on* a project *to* get *in*, not *project* that I had a project, how did that even happen, I guess it's just that midwestern niceness, goes much deeper than you could ever know I guess, nice people, they know so much, but don't say anything, except the niceness, man, I must be nice, always saying I've got something to show, and then never actually showing it, well I *had* something to show, but now got nothing to show for it, except now I guess yet another of life's *opportunities*, to sit here and rack my brain about how I am going to construct something *that is something*, with these somethings all around this room, and then I am going to take that something to somewhere, where some people are supposed to be, to say that this something made from some things brought somewhere *is something*, and then I'd be someone, man, sounds like a whole lot of nothing.

There was a knock at the door, thick and hearty, both the door and the knock, it startled T, but was at the same time welcomed, because now something else was happening.

guidance

"Yes, come right on in!" T said with an ignoble interest, as if there was plenty more room for others to be clueless.

"Hi, Professor Gershom, it is nice to meet you, I am from Calabaster, in the Literary Studies program there," a nervous voice was able to fit in saying all before opening the door clear enough to begin entering, which through its port a small but slender frame appeared, with some undersized clothes to match, except for the boots, those are oversized, but then the ankles to calves are fabricless, and then there is that sweater which is too big in the middle but the sleeves are way too short, nevermind, "Yes, how can I help you?" T said, not fully realizing what was just mis-confirmed, still watching a body attempting to fit through a door that was decisively not opened enough by its mind, an awkward entrance indeed.

T, sitting in the chair behind a desk which sat towards the back of the room with the desk facing the entrance, there was the bookshelf to the left which filled the wall until a small window which was just before the door opposite, from the corner, to it, and then in the other corner of the room was a small trophy-case, filled with different accolades, photos, potentially heirlooms, or souvenirs from expensive trips, a brown-leather couch, with a circle coffee table in front of it, and some mies van der rohe looking chairs across from that, the chairs sitting in front of the desk, are a more regal looking type, traditional office design, that T was now encouraging the student to sit in so that they could speak.

"Yes, hi, my name is Melissa," the student said before jutting out a stiff hand, as the sweater exposed the elbow for a brief moment, before sliding back to mid-forearm.

T took the hand, quite cold, but in the way that you don't think the person has been outside, but hiding, maybe, just hiding somewhere, away from the world, from themselves, from the surface of their own skin, so that when they use their limbs the energy lambaste from so much repression catapults like an ocean wave that recedes too quickly, so that with the next pulse it is crashing into its previous movement rather than into fluid movement, you know, the ones that make you think a big wave is coming then you stand there for fifteen minutes wondering what just happened and if the ocean is asleep, or perhaps too nervous to continue speaking, or pull her hand back, oh there it goes, "yes, hi, so I am actually really excited that you are here, I had asked some other people, and they said they heard from faculty that you hadn't returned yet from your sabbatical, but I thought maybe you had, and that you were in your office, and look here you are, how great!"

"How great!" T responded, with that same odd-enthusiasm from earlier, almost automatically, "Here *I* am," T said through a big, toothy grin.

"So, first I just wanted to say, your negative-equivalence theorem, is astounding, we were all amazed when we heard about it, well after we understood what it meant, but really, thank you, it is just such an exciting time to be within literary studies, who could have thought it was possible to introduce logic into literary studies, obviously that *Bart* guy got it wrong, he was still entrenched in the patriarchy, and gave no concern for how his signfied was just signifying its own phallogocentrism, he never did get out of the diegetical constraint as you call it, to see and say his theory *was his theory*, and then to modify it accordingly to what reality presently is so that, *through negative-equivalence*, you can understand the Real version, or at least that which is not not the Real but no longer just the Imaginary that had built the diegetical constraint in the first place.

Is that right?" Melissa said with a curious look, not that she thought she would have gotten it right, but she wanted to make sure Professor Gershom, I mean T, was approving of whatever she had said, the same look that fell upon the undergraduates when they were pushing T into the office, the guy saying how they wouldn't want to prevent knowledge from occurring, how important it is at conferences that everything goes *smoothly*, because it's all anyone ever talks about, they say the internet will one day take over, but I don't know how you'd get all the backroom dialogue out on stage on the internet, would probably have to be put in even further backchannels, and then you know how bad that can get, but it's all bad anyway, all of it, the look, the conceit, the concern, what is this knowledge occurring anyway, T looked down at the desk and opened a notebook to the page securely grasped, the first line said, "I could instead say this...", so T, decided squarely to instead say this:

"If we view a formalized logic as an abstracted form of reasoning concretized in the formalized language itself, then we could agree that this language is not the interior or personal language of any individual person or entity, but that instead the individual person or entity accesses the formal language through the *mediation* of their own interior or personal language, to parse out both the errors of the formalizing language process and any other way of constructing language that is not the formalized language."

T spoke in repose, unsure of what had even been said, not because T wouldn't understand something like this, but that because T did not know where it came from, how it existed, it just appeared there, knowledge, pure knowledge, how to speak pure knowledge, well apparently it is written, by this Professor Gershom, maybe I should keep reading it, "whereas," except that is what it had said, oof, I slipped the page, I don't think she noticed, she's looking like whatever I am going to say will be profound no matter what, wait, what does that say on the page it turned to, I *should* read this, "the negative-equivalence theorem is the means by which one contained within a system can get out, it is the underlying metaphor of my resistance or rebellion that sought the right to its own individuation.

Thus it is the prompt of all individuation, yet still lives as a phantom, for it is not realized what *it is* that has become until it does, and thus for now all still lives in the differentiated unity of 'all of this', and we beset to realize that all of 'all of this' is just some of this much larger 'all of this', and so on."

guidance

T read each word with great poise, as if at some point the voice of the text had taken on its own life and was speaking through T, even going so far as to make the air quotes.

Melissa sat contented, ready to absorb what had been spoken, ready to speak something to pass the moment into the next, yet T realizing a familiar word spoke with even greater enthusiasm, "*Whereas*, with the positive-infinity quandary it becomes more apparent how all is what it is as it is becoming what it is, thus there becomes no need for this spectre haunting of memory, instead all action need not *identify* but simply the means to become their Self."

Now T was really unsure of what had just been said.

Melissa looked down towards the page, and up at T, or Professor Gershom, with full tears running down her face, "That is the most beautiful thing I have ever heard, I cannot believe you have discovered that, that is going to change everything, please, *please*, I know it is the last day of the conference, and you are probably busy with getting settled back-in, but *it is* the last day of the conference," she said now with a rising confidence that seemed to inspire T, "you have to come and teach this positive-infinity quandary to the other students from Calabaster, please, we won't write or say anything about it, promise, it would just give us so much hope to know that you are going to publish it soon, we are just a few of us, I could go get them now," standing up, and turning towards the door she said with that same curious look.

"Oh no, that's not possible right now," T said with a startled-fluster, "I couldn't poss..."

"...you are busy right, *I did just barge in*," she said now with a remarkably deep sadness portrayed through those same eyes, the rest of the face did nothing to change the state of things, just the reflection of those eyes to whatever was just said, T couldn't handle it, not because of the eyes but because of the *double meaning*, not that *other* kind of double meaning, but because it puts me up here, I don't know what to say or do, I don't even know who I am, man.

"It's just I have a lot of work to do, I was supposed to finish a report for those three from the *other* University, the University of the Midwest, or in the Mid...er, uh I am going to be here until later working on..."

T started to pause, realizing there were no thoughts in that direction either.

"Oh later!" Melissa said with a re-inspired poise, "Should we come back *here* then," quickly attaching to the words she thought she heard the Professor say.

"Well...*actually*, I am not sure there are enough chairs!" T said with that odd-enthusiasm again, as if it would be a helpful thing to say in this moment, perhaps T was nervous as well...I am nervous, man, those eyes keep wavering on every shift of my face, I don't know which thought is going which way before I am already judging myself to know what it means, what I mean, "...what I mean to say, is I am not sure if this room would have enough space to fit all of your colleagues," T said, now a little more confident.

"That is not a problem!" Melissa said in quick response.

"We can use Conference Room A, or the *Integrity Stageroom*, I think that is what they call it here.

I looked at the schedule earlier and the *Interrogative Methods: Practical Reasoning within Discourse* seminar should be culminated by 6:30pm, so everyone will either be in B, or at the reception, which I think is in the restaurant or sports bar thing, whatever it is they have, I am not sure, I haven't...anyway, is that agreeable?" She said shifting again, I want to tell her whatever she was saying was okay, even though it's not being questioned, that it is was just the information that was hefty not the moment itself, but then again, I realize how hefty this moment really is, man, there could be a professor amongst those colleagues, and I could tell them it was all a misunderstanding and I am an assistant to Professor Gershom, or something like that, and maybe, since they are so enamored with this work over there, I can spend all afternoon learning, and then they can put in word I am looking for a post somewhere, and that is the fast-track you always hear about T, the skipping-the-line-move that really is what gets anybody anywhere, especially in academia these days, I think I should say yes.

"Yes, yes I find that agreeable," T said squarely, sitting up in the chair, to find the posture which allowed the chest to open the lungs and the back to be properly supported by the legs.

"I think I'll spend some time, even, preparing a small lecture for you and your friends."

2I

June 6th, 2012

Today started good, the streak was going well.

Raca, woke up this morning a new man, new clothes, *new haircut*, even washed his hands after every bathroom use, really commend the guy, this investigation *has been good for him.*

Well, that is, until the interview he just came back from, apparently...he was supposed to interview this Professor at the school, someone who taught a class similar to Professor Cinotau's, but this Professor Gershon *character* came in...in a huff, and demanded the right to be interviewed because they believed Professor Cinotau had not only prompted the students to revolt, but had done so by stealing the theories of Professor Gershom, which caused all of this drama because Gershom was senior faculty, very distinguished fella, and reminded this to Raca many times before the meeting, *and during*...and when Raca came back out the other Professor was gone, probably because of how rude Gershon was...which caused Raca to have a bit of a panic because he was supposed to get that interview...but now this Professor is insisting that he has to interview whoever...whomever was working at some conference five years ago, and the trial is tomorrow!

22

Trial - Opening Statements

Oh hey, you are here!

Well...I would welcome you but that is odd...I do not have anything to welcome you into...that is, the trial has not yet started...it is of some odd occurrence...that I seem to be *mis-aligned*, I would say I am outside of something, perhaps the narrative *or time itself*, but nonetheless, the Trial was supposed to be held all on one day, June 7th, so that everyone could digest the event in one moment, it would have been *way too much* to have it over separate days, the parents were starting to get rowdy about it because they were *just* hearing about it from the kids, even though the kids had been talking about it for weeks, and as you know how those things go, nobody really *wants* to be the kid that has to explain to the parent what the thing is that is not a thing anymore but it was a thing that you had to be there for, so it's awkward nonetheless when you *do* describe it that it's not actually *the* thing anymore, but this half-thing, a hybrid of the original thing and the version of the thing that is instantaneously being manifested through a performance of 'the thing', that is not *the* thing, but the only person who knows it's not *the* thing is the person who is performing it, or those who, too, awkwardly watch as this monster-thing is being performed for a group of people who have *already* formed their bias about what it is from *what they've heard*, creating meta-folds on the hybridization of this ever-growing *thing* that is not *the* thing, or if they are impartial are being informed about the *thing* by the *performance* of not *the* thing, so there is not much reason to assume they would have any idea what anybody was talking about, and so, so many parents had no idea what anybody was talking about, and they heard a lot of *things* that they *thought* they understood, but were just a collection of *not*-things that their minds were clamoring in support of with their bodies, so the administration started to fold under the constant stress of having more than a handful of Felix and Bens, Martha and Marys congregating in front of the school, causing the town to start asking questions that could lead to a *real* news team arriving, which was the main fear of the administration, always, at any point, *that a real news team would arrive*, unplanned that is, they did every *thing* they could to prepare for the event so that no matter what 'the thing', there would always be a good shot in the background for the news van to pan over with the camera, to establish ground for the not *the* thing, and then if anything that had happened *happened* in any of the classrooms there was always a good lake view so that nobody could avoid saying to themselves, *wow that's a nice view*, and to insure that nobody *ever* intercepted the news team before they arrived to investigate any word that had gotten out, the administration was always ready, *photo-ready*, in their offices to show how hard they were working on whatever matter, no matter what it was, because then with the announcement of the news team the dissemination of strategy was so efficient the school *always controlled the narrative.*

That is what I was able to determine, in some *way*, because unfortunately for me, they kept me outside, probably because Raca cannot keep me inside, he can't really keep anything *inside*, he has been non-stop crying this morning, he was sobbing most of the night too, but he got better at some point...that stupid doofus...Raca thought he was going to see him today and started crying just thinking about the horror of being harassed by that *doofus* again...but in front of my bosses, respectful people don't cry...how could he cry in a courtroom, he thought, they are *televised*, and somebody will be in the corner drawing his picture, *him crying*, and the audience will think that he is guilty because *he is the one crying*, at the opening statements no less, talk about *guilt*, he kept telling himself that if he cried he would be guilty, that if he cried he would be guilty, he kept telling himself that throughout the opening statements.

23

Home Part I

"How was your weekend?"

"*Huh?*"

"Nevermind, did you have *anything* on your mind that you wanted to talk about?" Professor Dillinger said to Professor Cinotau after he was let into the home.

"Well, that's always true," Professor Cinotau said, walking ahead of Professor Dillinger towards a chair in the living room to sit.

On the wall behind the chair sat what looked like an original painting, *a relief no less*, that had a deep horizon producing a stunning lake in the background, it looked like the lake in Vedici but from a more southern angle.

Even through its physical design, a wood-cut board with insets to give features and depth to the objects painted, it had a surrealistic feel to it, that sense that some existential disaster is unfolding, as two individuals are depicted, one standing at the end of staircase jutting into the sky from the shore to meet the sun setting on the horizon flush with the line of the last step, and the other individual rests near the base of the staircase looking at these tidal ponds that hold the deepness of galaxies, except for the one being observed and in it lies a small starfish.

Next to the painting sat a small white placard.

Similar to the one you'd find in a modern museum, except upon closer detail it looks like it was actually just printed out on paper, and not *some material*.

It reads: "The dialectician laments, *there is no step beyond*, to which the metaphysician exclaims, *There is!* — a work by Progressive Thought"

"Do you get many guests?" Professor Dillinger said looking at the placard before standing near the window.

"Alone in my exile, at rest—behest, detest, and unquest...well that is, except for you!"

24

1:35 pm - Sunday

T was sitting again at the desk, after having snuck out earlier for some food T had returned with a peanut butter and chocolate hazelnut spread sandwich, not anything that had been prepared already, but not far down the hall from Professor Gershom's office, that is if you go left when you exit, that is after walking down the hallway, because if you went directly left you'd go through the corridor wall and fall out of the building, but if you walk the corridor of offices, Gershom's sits at the end, which is why it has the window right by the door, but if you extend that wall about fifty feet you have the whole corridor of the fourth floor in the *Andresen-Hus*.

There are offices reflecting the windows in the hallway, since they have no windows inside it seems the doors were usually kept open, and at the end of the corridor is a staircase which takes you up or down only, really, the building is as uniform a *building* as a building could be, 80x30x80, stairs, check, hallways with windows, check, offices, check, but it was hailed as an achievement in academic architecture, really, they had said they had defied some type of limit they thought wasn't possible, but I think they may have just been fibbing, because above the fourth floor was the breakroom, which took up the whole floor, no interior walls, just a skylight glass ceiling, no windows in the walls, four round tables, a wet bar, it was a faculty building no less, but maybe it's not something I get, I couldn't even find the bathroom, maybe because I've never gotten on the otherside, but anyway, if you go left when you get to the staircase, on each floor is dry pantry, and this one happened to have some fixings, so I helped myself, just like I will help myself to some more of this knowledge, pure, abstract, *knowledge*, let's see, let's look again at this tear-jerking quote.

T laughed while taking a bite of the sandwich, reaching for the notebook from earlier, which this time had a piece of paper from elsewhere on the desk stuffed in to make sure that the page had not gotten lost, the paper was some sort of brochure about the *15 Best Things to Do While in Italy*, that most likely had been left behind, perhaps decidedly, before a trip abroad, perhaps the sabbatical, okay, now the detective mind is going, let's see what this all says, T thought, looking at the page from earlier, reading it over again, now with a determined confidence that these are T's words, not for any sense of plagiarising them *as* T's words, but that these words, as they are being spoken are being spoken *as if* T is rewriting them, tracing over them in the mind, so that they might *as well* have been spoken, spoken as, spoken for, speaking with, speaking to, to the sensibility of the sentiment and sense of the prose, to find its meter and voice, to listen to its hypertensions, and attitudes, to give it form, this was T's speciality really, this is why the Conference was even a reasonable destination in the first place, T didn't have this plan initially, promise, the plan would have been to come here and get on board with one of the review committees for the week's lectures, it was likely that T would have been needed because of the snow, and while they normally would not allow anyone last minute, T had somewhat of a reputation for being able to digest information quickly and synthesize it for the present audience, which is why when T first started getting hired as a reviewer for the Conference, in the first couple of years, before they established their politics amongst the continued learning groups until it was that only *their people* could officiate the process, as it was *for their purposes anyway*, anyway, T was an outsider, so outside they pushed, encouraged really, T, to become a teacher at Vedici High, rather than attempt at the College, or even Copper's, but that was obvious considering how much some of the teachers made there, they told T that they needed someone there that could *bridge the gap, it was getting competitive up on the hill and all of the opportunities weren't trickling down like they used to*, the students at Copper's were coming up with newer and more innovative experiments and projects that were taking on more of the town's funding, and considering that the town was basically self-governed, except for a governor that would come every so often to cut another ribbon, or congratulate another international accolade, somehow always forgetting that there were *two high schools*, in Vedici, always mentioning how *the* high school is a shining example for all other towns on what can be done with a motivated and politically-savvy town, when parents stop getting scared by what's on a tax form and starts using them to scare the government, the governor would always say and laugh pointing at one dad or another that stood on stage for

a reason only a handful of people knew, anyway, let's see
what this Gershom had to say next, it's already getting late.

On the next page, from earlier, this was written:

"They've taken over my mind"

"It's just the words that exist"

"All else is dreams"

"They are just trying
to get me to
say it"

"...to
make
it
public
what
needs
to
be
known:

there is no such thing as
positive *memory*"

The next page, after, held another brief remark:

> "Fallacy: to say that we are to transvaluate for the *sake* of *new* values...
>
> yet Eternal Return is just the confirmation of this already lived life *again*"

Intrigued, but not yet able to grasp onto something, T kept reading further, especially so because more familiar words started to appear again, on the next page:

> "What Nietzsche is after is nothing less than pure affirmation itself, that which claims not that its differences have made it superior to what can be called worse, but instead its *own* identity, affirmed, a novel becoming of itself, a word, an idea, a statement, a memory, a dream, all coming to mean, what they are as themselves rather than how they are in relation to what they could potentially be, thus in contra-counter-super-imposition to the negative-equivalence theorem *is* the positive-infinity quandary:
>
> Being being being being Being
>
> For where does the subject *actually* exist?

It continues:

awakening

"For Nietzsche sought to understand at what point does the divine live in reality, for up until this point we can only ever view reality from the point of our perspective, there becomes no where else to move, but instead to discover or create *an exit*, a means by which the divine can be discovered so that we can create a bridge into its way of being.

> What comes out from a perspective seeking to find within itself a truth it does not possess?
>
> -an *other* abyss

This is the positive-infinity quandary, that any idea in support of its truth, or any based in that assumption, would precede to become determined only by the provability of its own determination—the positive-infinity.

Thus rather than derail, with the mathematics of the Grelling paradox—instead I seek to mention how it means, plainly:

> We cannot learn what we do not know, we only can dream memory, but what we know has *always been*, created by our dreamed up memory and thus we have the false illusion that we have control, therefore we know nothing and can learn nothing, without having even learned *it*.

For it is by default by not knowing anything, *that* we could only know nothing.

But this like any other theory stands to reason itself as what *it* means, thus you must realize how I have trapped the page inside of itself, filled it up so to speak, so that it could become a resource of action for the being of itself within the becoming of the earth, for it lives thus it is and so it is a part of all being as *it* becomes to exist, but is not anything for it is nothing, and further yet it has no becoming despite *now* becoming to exist, thus like a seed it has been caught abreast in the winds of our world, thus there must be a reason it is that I can reach this point, yes I must be very close..."

It was last the page in the notebook that had writing, except for the next page which had a date...*from three years prior*.

"Great, a solution unwritten for a problem unwriteable, yet so remarkable that it brought a young woman to tears," T said, reclining in the chair as hands, interlaced, supported the head, "I think I am even *further* from having something to say than earlier, even if I had my research, it might not even matter at this point," T started laughing, a little too loud for comfort, but the hallway was empty and no one had been in the other offices, T had checked, T had checked the whole building really, was hoping someone else *would* be in the building, that someone else had miraculously appeared now, like that Melissa, so that some more sense could be made, because T did much better when things were moving, not sitting so stationary staring up from the page asking to be explained when it *itself* is calling *itself* unexplainable.

25

Eleventh Class

"Class is not meeting here, today. Please go to the museum at your own expense." Tommy read from a note posted on the door.

26

Trial - Prosecution's Argument with Evidence

Here you are, just in time!

The prosecution is just about to start its argument in response to witness testimony...the prosecution...but before we can get there, we have to get here, *first*, I mean, *I* am not yet there, we are still driving, pulling into the parking lot, *2B* this time, must hurry!

Raca ran through the security corridor towards the main quadrangle, nobody else was in the administration's building, but you can be damn sure he *did the flick*.

Given the parents request to be present, and be given turns to speak, *that is*, through the elected representational official for each of the continued learning groups, yes, *representational*, they only got the turn to speak for that day *representationally, given how many other opportunities some of the parents and professors get to speak, the parents that don't should be allowed to speak, and how the different groups have such different opinions, even among*...on, and on, and on...so the administration chose to allow five of the continued learning groups present, as a result of their own student's involvement in the course, to elect officials, *the chosen parents*, to speak, it is not clear why they were chosen, but nonetheless the group felt satisfied with *who was* selected, enough, that they didn't object any further and started to congregate around these individuals, in some-sort of narrative-agenda where those parents who *both* related to and saw a viable means to affect the trial in relation to their own concern towards its outcome in the plight of the elected official stood by that individual, and those that didn't understand that nuance of social cohesion stood near who they liked, or they didn't care, which is odd for such a scandalous event, but, yup, there you go, one dad just needed *to take a quick call*.

So the audience was comprised, sitting on the grass in their burgeoning franchisements ready to appeal to the interest of themselves, so that they could determine through a jury what the proper treatment and outcome of the events should be, the administration seemed to have deemed this an important occasion because they brought the red folding chairs out instead of the green ones.

Their seating was different, the faculty that is, somebody, probably a student or another, had constructed a stage, it was made of those steel-frames, not the ones you use for a building, *obviously*, but those ones that construct a whole frame of a stage, and then you put the boards on top of the frames, so that you now have a stage that is four inches off of the ground...yeah, I think a student constructed that, probably for a grade...but behind that they pulled those neat bleachers that butterfly-open to make a much longer row, they are really good for storage, but, anyway, the faculty was sitting on those, behind the stage, which had, *which was actually impressive*, somebody must have carried an antique desk out of one of the buildings, *and then*, did it again, because they were both stacked on the middle of the stage, with a stool behind them, and a replica-gavel on top.

There's our hero!

Just now they are bringing a regal looking chair, one of those traditional office design types, and putting it on the stage next to the double-desk, it isn't a student by the way, it seems that they gave *this job* to one of the cafeteria employees, the design most likely one of the administrators's, I am sure sitting in those *Hollywood Square* offices gets to your sense of decorum after a while.

Oh, off they go, back towards the entrance of the campus, they turned right before the security gate, they must be going off-shift, *or to their real shift.*

Well, anyway it seems like that has allowed the prosecution to begin, because now they are asking that the witnesses are told to be attentive and ready, they are waiting in the nearby chemlab, or what is left of it, one of the student-managers had left *early* to go out with some friends, almost a year back and had left a gas valve on, and one thing led to the next, and well, the chemlab is what they are calling the space where the witnesses are being attentive and ready.

The judge is being called in now as well, well, asked respectfully to come out from the *Andresen-Hus*, you know, I am sorry if I sound clueless about all of this, but since I missed the opening statements, I missed a lot of how this trial is supposed to occur, so I am not really sure what is supposed to occur...oh the judge is back, it's Professor Gershom, *neat*.

Professor Gershom is now walking out of the building and, with a bit of a grimace, looking towards the stage, and, yeah, with a big, reluctant sigh sitting on the stool, this will be great.

They've asked Raca to come out as the first witness, he is walking from the chemlab, fortunately it is one of the features of a building that was not considered part of the *lake view count*, and so it's relatively close to the ground.

Here he comes, from around where the bend first snakes around, he must have been in the building behind the one behind the stage, if that helps.

Our hero has returned, *from earlier*, with two tables from the cafeteria on a rolling cart, and some of the nicer, *not chairs* chairs, from the cafeteria, the ones that have plastic that feels like it was designed to reflect well in the photo of the new cafeteria but not in any other capacity of function.

They are asking Raca to sit in the chair next to the double-desk.

He looks really nervous, like he's looking around for something, he probably thinks that gawky kid is going to come out and flash a photo of him or say something mean, but luckily for him the administration *is way less* confident in its ability to handle the students than they are the parents, so all the students were told to stay home, and any of their response towards the events will be made discoverable through the testimony of their parent, you know, you could say that this was ill-designed, but, you could also have known that someone could say that too.

"This quite an ill-designed stage, and process," Professor Gershom said to the adoration of no one present.

"Well, let us begin, shall we, now can we have the prosecution state itself as present for the case of Cinotau vs the People of Vedici, and list the crimes being presented before the court for review and judgement please."

At the table on the right, sits the prosecutor, which just got finished being placed successfully, the table that is, which is what most people were paying attention to, *you know everyone says that it takes a village or whatever when you are trying to get something hard done, but they made that a lot harder than it needed to be*, one of the parents said to our hero, who just looked back, *uncomfortably*.

I have not seen this individual before, the prosecutor, *the hero* I am pretty sure works in the cafeteria, at the *fajita* section and that they do live in Vedici but down the hill, not too far from the lake actually, as there is some reasonable property down at the base level, it's actually an outlier on that property-value map, *from earlier*, because the land where our hero is from is in that sweet spot that is close enough to the forest grove so it still gets access to that county road which runs its perimeter, which can take you right downtown really, much faster than some of the neighborhoods closer in town, they have all of those yields, and the yellow stop signs, I don't know what those are, but neither do the kids, I don't think they know what the red ones are either, probably why they installed the yellow ones, but anyway, it is also near the lake, which keeps going south along the forest grove, and nobody tells anyone really, no one says it out of fear that if it is spoken it will get ruined, so I'll whisper instead, *it's the best part of the lake,* the sand hasn't been refined to a complete powder to appease the soft-footed so that it burns you anytime the sun is out, the water laps into waves in many spots because of the streams that connect from the forest grove, there are actually animals, not those squirrels that definitely have social security numbers, that you see either in the market square or by *Bender's Beach,* the hip, locale where for three times the price you can have two times worse quality food, next to the seagulls that are negotiating labor parties by the trash cans with the squirrels, to determine who gets what food where.

The prosecutor, named Miriam, who is Raca's boss, apparently, is now getting up from their chair and walking towards the bench, well the end of the platform, stage thing, it seems they are making a request, I don't know if the prosecutor is *actually* a prosecutor, in the sense that they went out and hired a prosecutor, but it might be someone's parent who filled the time, that or an academic, it is not like I would know, I spend most of my time at an abandoned chicken farm, and when it does come time for these things, Raca locks me out of his mind, as if he needs to concentrate, which, sure he needs to concentrate, but I don't understand how that is concentration unless he is literally concentrating *on concentration.*

They've, whoever they is here, and really, I am not trying to be so nondescript, I just can't hear anything from where I am, okay, I don't *want* to say it, but in case you were wondering I am not sitting in the audience.

No, no, I am not somebody, I am just the narrative voice, of whomever's narrative it is we are following, and for some reason, I am here.

...On *this* page, oh, for a brief moment, wow this is weird.

I had no idea, really, that this whole time I was the text inside of a book, perhaps I should have been aware of that earlier, I don't know if I have said very nice things.

I hope I have given a fair account of all of the events that have transpired, oh, oh it's done okay I can sit back down.

Raca sat back down, they just had him sworn-in, they've requested that he would do so first and then they asked that he'd be the one to make the presence of the prosecution known, it seems with that I am able to remain more present so I will step back from this trial of the absurd, and try to form the real one now.

Raca is now standing, *facing the parents*, at the end of the stage, as if he finally got the part in the school play and is now going to start the show off, "Hello everyone!" he yells very loudly, as if the loudness of his voice reflected the amount of people present and not the distance of its projection.

"The prosecution is present...before the court," he read from a sheet of paper in front of him, "within this...hereby initiated...trial...of...occurrence...towards...the state of affairs of the college of Hillbrandt...I, use na...I, Raca, stand before the court," he stood for a second looking at the page, and then turned around, "I, Raca, stand *before* the court, with the following accusation...and list of charges..in the case of Cinotau...vs...the people of Vedici," he said to no effect from the audience, but with the complete affect of his body, nerves shaking limbs like crazy.

"Tarrin Cinotau," who just became present at the defense's table, it seems Professor Cinotau was waiting in the *Andresen-Has*, and just arrived after being summoned by some gawky-student, who now Raca was looking at as his voice started to calm the frenetic timbre, before immediately switching through to a stressed vibrato as the words are being forced out with a graceful rage, "Professor of Letters and Motions at Hillbrandt College is being accused of the following offenses against the sanctity and sanity of this dear and precious institution: Producing extreme views on the importance of maintaining a relationship with the mainstream canon of public opinion, encouraging students to go off *on their own*, which can result in complete dissension or disillusion towards the sacred and common good of all people; progenitor of emotional seminars producing extreme moments of criticality against the status quo of reality so as to allow students to dis-situate themselves from the history of their education and stand on their own, potentially causing them to no longer *fit in* in the larger society of people," the crowd cheered at some points, they seemed to take strongly to seeing a member of the administration standing before them and saying what was on their mind, finally, they thought, "for these accusations we find that only the most extreme judgement of the measures of the penal code of Hillbrandt College be referenced and utilized in this manner, beset to the discretion of the Jury."

Now the crowd really cheered, as Raca sat back down in the regal chair.

"First to the stand, we ask...whichever parent wants to go...you okay, first to the stand we ask Parent #1," the prosecutor said in a soothing tone, her voice was not upsetting, that you would normally be thinking a prosecutor would be, but she sounded like that grade administrator who always understood the student's problems, talking it out and laughing with them about each aspect of it, right before telling them that their parents were on the way and that they were suspended.

Lucky, chosen contestant Parent #1 is somebody's dad, it would be helpful if we had a way to know *whose dad*, but who would know whose dad is this?

"Whose dad are you?" asked the prosecution.

"I'm Maddie's dad," oh okay, that was helpful, apparently.

"Okay Mis..Maddie's dad, has Maddie properly informed you of what she believes to have transpired the day of the event in question."

"Excuse me, could you please state the event in question," some parent from the audience yelled, "it's necessary for basic grounds of discovery to properly occur or else the evidence cannot be associated to the discernment of the event," I think it's the dad on the cellphone, yeah, he's just yelling legal advice, well, no, now he's back to talking on the cell phone, some other parents agreed.

"Maddie's dad," the prosecutor began again, slightly annoyed, "are you able to talk about, *what Maddie talked about*, when she talked about the event in question, which is the occurrence of twenty-two children seen fleeing from a classroom towards the campus exit."

"Certainly, little *Madster* told me the whole scoop," oh, no, not one of *these dads*, did he really just say that, did they really select this guy, his attitude matches his double-collar.

"Well, would you mind sharing with the court what it is li..Mads...Maddie said," you can tell this dad is getting to her too.

"Well..here's what she said...her and her friends were taking this class because there was this cool Professor, not like the other professors, yah know, and they thought it would be more about magic stuff because they heard rumors about the teacher...and what do yah know long story short the rumors are true, the magic stuff happened and we are all here."

"I am sorry, sir, but that is not admissible as testimony," Professor Gershom said to the dad that had started to get up, "you cannot just truncate what it is that happened with *'long story short'*, we need to hear that long story *long*," said, Gershom, again, to the adoration of no one present.

"Come on...what more could you want, I'm giving you all I got," the dad said back to Professor Gershom, doing that *thing* where he slaps the back of his hand over the palm of the other with each word, as if they suddenly mean more.

"Let me try something...your honor," the prosecutor said to a now all-too-pleased Gershom. "Sir, when Maddie told you that the events took place, I mean, that 'the magic stuff happened', what is it that she said *had* happened?"

"I don't know."

"You don't know what she said or you don't know what I am asking?"

"What do you want?"

"What? I am just asking for you to answer the question."

"I don't know what question you want me to answer."

"*What* happened?"

"I DON'T KNOW!" the dad now yelled, his wife came quickly to the stage in his defense, but apparently he actually doesn't know anything...*Maddie doesn't tell him anything.*

"My turn!" shouted the parent, *apparently* next, two-collars had now gone back to his car, his wife stayed to find out what is going on, he's going to play with the radio.

"Okay, and we have here joining u..."

"I'm Maple Marbello, Martina's mom," she said to great effect, either this Martina must have been well-known or this Mom makes a mean reputation for herself in this town.

"Thank you Maple, I would like to ask you the same question, are able to speak on behalf of your daughter, Martina, on behalf of her behalf of the events transpired?"

"Yes, I came prepared," she said taking a quick pause, "*I talked to* my daughter," face deadpan looking over the audience just before curling into a look of faux-self-shame, she's got them laughing, she knows she's good, damn.

"And what is it that Martina told you?"

"Well, I want to be very clear, here, my Martina would never have done anything wrong, so she may not have seen the events as clearly as other parents' kids, but at least she saw it *and told me about it*," she did it again, they're still laughing.

"Yes, and what did she tell you," the prosecutor said a bit too early, you know before the audience calmed down, you could tell Maple noticed.

"She told me that all of the students started screaming and ran out of the classroom," she said turning into a pose towards the audience, they all clapped automatically, "There had been some lesson plan that had gotten one of the students very freaked out, and it freaked out one of the other students, and they freaked out one of the other students, and...and you know how it goes," half-turn, hand on cheek, smile, another applause.

"Do you know what the lesson plan had the students doing, you know, that caused them to *freak out*."

"No I am not sure."

"Did Martina?"

"She wasn't sure, she wasn't entirely there, she was..."

"...did your daughter attend the class, m'am?"

"...well yes, of course she did! It's just that..."

"...was your daughter late to class, m'am?"

"No, she was not late! Martina would not be late!"

"Well, where was she when the lesson plan was unfolding."

"She was on the other side of the room...okay!"

"Okay, m'am, whatever you want to say before the court."

"She was not late!...and it's not like being late was ever a crime," three-quarters turn, head-tilt, hands on hips, hip-jut she's got them back, they are all laughing again.

Seems like it was good time for her exit, Ms. Marbello gave a quick bow and went back to her seat to the adoration of several of her seatmates.

"Okay could we have the next witness, then" the prosecutor said to Professor Gershom who was distracted by the audience, who seemed to be distracted by itself, as the parents had now started talking amongst themselves, it had been happening progressively over the course of the last testimony, that is with each joke more and more people kept making small talk with their neighbors, probably to spread the energy, *and to be nice,* and they all fell into little conversations asking careful questions that are then being immediately returned and dissected with surface-observations, it doesn't seem like their attention is coming back anytime soon."

"Okay, this is not working," the prosecutor now said to Gershom's surprise, as she was standing right next to the double-desk.

"Could we move forward to reviewing the evidence?"

"Yes, I think that would be best," Gershom said softly, before slamming the replica-gavel onto the desk several times.

The parents seemed to already half-know they were doing something they shouldn't, because they were not startled by the sound of the gavel, but lowered their hum temporarily to then pick it back up in certain spots, with more spots picking up, *because if they are not going to listen why should we.*

The gavel struck the desk three more times, before its head fell off, and a very embarrassed Gershom chased it off the stage to only fall off after reaching for it at the edge.

Raca just helped Gershom up, and found the lost object and you can tell his face is starting to get *frustra*..."Everyone shut up! We need to complete this can't you see that you are preventing the trial from happening!" Raca yelled at the now quiet parents.

"Okay, thank you, Raca," the prosecutor said, now with that same soothe in her voice as earlier, "Let us begin reviewing the evidence that has already been submitted to the court. First I would like to bring attention..."

"Wait, a minute!"

"Yes?"

"I would like to speak."

"What do you mean," asked a confused prosecutor to a, now, bright-eye Gershom.

"Well, now that everyone warmed-up, I mean is ready," Professor Gershom said where just only the prosecutor could hear.

"Okay, *if you want* to make a statement then this would be the time," the prosecutor said stepping back to their table.

"Hello everyone, it is actually in great appreciation that we regard your presence with us today.

I would like to let you all know that we have heard all of your complaints, *well enough today*, and also through all of your various methods of correspondence.

We are well aware of what occurred during the events in question, and for that we do not need to spend *too* much time reviewing the evidence.

There is a greater problem afoot, that has arisen in the past day, that it has become of supreme importance to the court to bring to attention for you now.

You see, our dear Professor Cinotau, *here*, did much more than rambunct a group of students, Professor Cinotau has been academically defrauding the entire institution since arriving here."

The audience was aghast, that one dad has momentarily put his phone down, you could see that Professor Cinotau was starting to get uncomfortable, for most of the day now had just been sitting, in that pose known all too well, eyes forward but not focused, face relaxed but not fixed, ears attentive but not listening, mind aware but not thinking, *zen,* 'that way *zen* everyone keeps bothering me I can keep it', T would repeat as a mantra, mulling over whether or not it was a good pun, T liked to do that *as the mantra*, T liked to do odd things, but T did not like what was just said.

27

5:55 pm - Sunday

For that some *thing*, something was done, that is, T sat in Professor Gershom's office, leafing through every book, and other notebook that could be found, even reading the travel brochure, all in a hopes of finding something else that could spark a sense of reason, 'just the smallest spark' T kept saying in low hums while looking through the texts, if only something could be said that would give me something to say, but nothing or nobody is here, and I can't shake the feeling that this is the moment I actually lose it all, that all these times I've put myself into the narrow straits to come out unscathed and capable of what others didn't believe, or didn't want to believe, it'll all be for naught, it always is isn't, when the big nothing finally shows up it obliterates everything before it, nothing that happened in the past can stop the great nothing from arriving, that is, that is, wait a minute, I remember something here, in one of these Nietzsche books it was written, T started scrambling backwards into the mountain of books that were out on the floor, which had been occupying T for most of the afternoon.

There in the pile of books was a copy of *Nietzsche's Thought of Eternal Return* by Joan Stambaugh, probably the best out of the bunch T thought, this Stambaugh character sure knows how to synthesize, can take whole histories of narrative and condense it to one paragraph for the sake of showing how one or two arguments influenced the whole history unbeknownst to itself, writing with the truth of humanity as the priority, a true Nietzschean indeed, perhaps it might be helpful to read the dust jacket description:

> "Despite the common realities of modern technological advances, the thought of eternal return remains the most enigmatic concept to the Western mind. Recurrence and transmigration—central ideas in Eastern thought—have had only a small place in Western philosophy, Friedrich Nietzsche, however, was deeply concerned with the doctrine of eternal return, and although his critics and biographers have largely ignored his work on it, Nietzsche himself considered it his most important.
>
> Drawing from all of the German philosopher's writings, including his unpublished work, Joan Stambaugh has constructed a unified analysis of the thought of eternal return. She explores the extent to which Nietzsche was influenced by the idea of cyclical time dominant in Greek philosophy and by the concept of rebirth present in much of Eastern thought. Many important passages from Nietzsche are here translated into English for the first time.

The author examines the thought of eternal return by isolating its three components: eternity, return or recurrence, and the same or the self. She states that although the terms return and recurrence occur indiscriminately in Nietzsche, the distinction is an important one since it allows for several interpretations of his thought. The question is essentially whether what returns is the "same" series of behavior events, or some kind of self.

The way Nietzsche described the moment when this vision-like thought occurred to him (or, as he says, "invaded" him) suggest that eternal return was for him primarily a matter of his own experience, something which he "saw" but could never fully grasp. His statements on eternal return are insolubly contradictory and they cannot be reconciled within his own frame of reference, which is conditioned by the traditional metaphysical dualism of subject-object prevalent since Descartes. Thus, after presenting the various theories of eternal return in Nietzsche's writings, Joan Stambaugh discusses the influence of Eastern philosophy on his thinking. She then develops her own independent theories of time and eternity, occurrence and recurrence."

Quite a book indeed, T thought, this will have what I need, wait there it is that I remember, a subsection titled, *The Significance and Implications of Nietzsche's "There is No End" for a Theory of Time"*, this should say something about the big nothing, let me read it:

> To repeat, these are ideas that Nietzsche touched on, but whose implications he never developed. Without knowing it, he came very close to a Buddhist theory of time which was apparently never discovered by his "Eastern" mentor Schopenhauer. Schopenhauer was concerned with the cycles of birth, death, and rebirth central to the mythology of early Buddhism and to Brahmanism. Nietzsche somehow gained experience of the instantaneity of time and then partially attempted to reinterpret it in terms of the cycles familiar to him, above all Schopenhauer.
>
> It is neither possible nor necessary to develop this theory of time completely in order to understand Nietzsche's thought of eternal return. The most basic insight of Nietzsche's thought concerns the non-finality of time, and we shall limit ourselves to the implications of that insight rather than plunge into the intricacies of Buddhism. One might even say that part of Nietzsche's emphasis on eternal

return as a *thought* was born of his realization that he had not completely penetrated his own experience. He somehow seemed to know that eternal return was yet to be really *thought out.* Thus he presented it as a doctrine still to be fathomed and was very concerned about the effect it might have, particularly on the higher types of humans.

Yet we must at least mention briefly the Buddhist concepts of samsara and nirvana again in this context, for they are central to the problem of "no end." Whereas the West takes an infinity of time (eternity as endless time) to be something desirable and "positive," the East regards an infinity of time (the endlessly recurring cycles of samsara) as something full of suffering and "negative," particularly since a profound ignorance (avidya) is linked to these cycles. If a Westerner is asked whether they prefer annihilation in death or eternal life, they will probably choose the latter. An Easterner would say (as did Plato with an entirely different emphasis in the *Phaedo*) that there is no annihilation in death. Life follows upon death, just as death follows upon life. Therefore, "eternal life" in the Eastern sense means endlessly recurring world cycles, not some beatific transcendent state. One cannot, so to speak, catapult out of the dimension of birth and death to some other state without a profound transformation of consciousness. Physical death cannot alter that dimension. This profound transformation of consciousness leads to nirvana, the enlightened release from endlessness; yet it *is* at the same time this nirvana. Nirvana is the only way out of unknowing endlessness. There is no "automatic" annihilation in death. Nirvana is not annihilation; it is an enlightened ending.

T sat rereading over the last few lines, saying them again and again until they sunk in, "Nirvana is the only way out of unknowing endlessness," great, my answer is right there T, thought said, to T who just kept saying it again, and again, T, man, we went from needing a non-solution for a problem we didn't know existed to needing to transcend both, how are you not laughing at this, T?

T stood up and looked at the door just as a capricious knock landed upon it.

I am not sure, let's follow after, T just went out the door towards it rather than allowing it to come in, I am not sure why, wait, it's half-past six, that must be the students, they are going to give the lecture, wait, T, oh, wait, I get it now.

"There *is* no answer! Only the answer *is*!" T said to a mind trailing behind, "it's only a moment that is needed, and this *is a moment*."

28

Trial - Defense's Statement with Evidence

"You mean to say something like *induction,* don't you Professor Cinotau?"

"Well, reframe how I said what I said with how you think what I said *is* what I said, and I will be, by all means, capable of seeing if that is true."

"Well, you said that for all of human history we have only been able to determine what things are insofar as we are able to determine what is not us determining them *as determinable,* and thus we have been a history of innities or errors within which we stepped into the pants of the previous generation without realizing in order to conceptualize our own becoming within the reality *we believed* we were becoming, but were only insofar as we were upholding the mantle of perspectiving the reality from our ontic-position within the Imaginary.

Therefore, you suggested that it may be possible to, rather, be *told* what it is that is what *is,* not in a way that suggests *something* for what is and determines what 'what is' *really is,* but to just implicitly *know* what it is that is 'what is', as I see it, that would be induction."

"Yes, as you *see it* indeed, but that is the difficulty of seeing isn't it, that for induction to occur we need to both tag and code 'what is' for the determinability of such an affective position, that we have to recognize that often times the occurrence of the tagging is the belief you have just inspired, but the actual coding of that which has been tagged is determinable to its own structure which necessarily necessitates a structure thereby incurring the phenomenality of the coding which if bound to some fixity will not be possible as an ontic-positionality of impartiality towards a schematization which fits its own ontic-identity—rather the complex that would be necessitated, would be necessitated to re-form for any new occurrence of itself thus re-writing what previous efforts have already occurred rather than dynamically adapting what it is that is occurring.

I am not interested in accumulation and that is precisely the matter at hand, I am not interested in collecting things, rather I want them to *be* collectivized, *into* the accumulation of perspective that is occurring within the experience of their collectivization, for it is the activity of that space which over time will produce an understanding of the fluidity of concept within which I will then be able to speak for *what* 'what is' *is.*

The problem of induction is that it cannot exist without defining the concept first, and thus it cannot exist without defining the concept first if it does not have some method of rehypothecation by which it delays the authority of the definition until it can be said to fit into some model of arrangement suitable for collective interpretation.

What I am suggesting is a way of *knowing* that by doing something, *over time*, the knowledge of what that something is will become clearer and clearer, and that this clarity, if properly captured will produce a strain of logic which could be said to be the logical formation of that something over the time that it becomes knowable, and thus would be a proof of the thing-itself, which much like how art captures reality and thus further photos capture the process of capturing and then the digital captures everybody for the virtual is an infinite abyss, it is that I have found a way to capture the truth of things becoming themselves, as if I were able to see what was going on within the *infamous box* without opening it.

This way is precisely defined by a method of rigidity which allows for the belief to occur that it is possible, but in the actual doing of the method it is that the belief is sufficient, for the theory allows for believing action to be the only necessity for the active participant to be able to determine some relationality to the event of the knowledge coming to be known, and thus from there we can assist this active participant with certain referent schematizations which will allow them to orient reality in such a way that its infinite complexity aligns to allow for pockets of clarity which give sense to an undergirding sentiment that when revealed becomes the focal point of a temporality of introspection by which they *could* become capable of arriving at truth, and if they utilize the methods of the theory to treat this experience and their own perspective of it, my argument, is that over time they will be able to align their own belief in knowing that the coming to know knowledge is possible *with* the coming to know the knowledge itself—which would be confirmed by the arrival of the knowledge itself.

So no, I don't think you ever *understood* the positive-infinity quandary, because induction would never be the solution."

"So then how, do you propose to suggest it is that we are *ever* capable of doing this, why is it that we *can* do this, rather than *cannot*, essentially, how is it that we are having this conversation now, *with sense*?"

"We had lost ourselves completely..."

"What do you mean?"

"We did not know where it is that we *as* a Self is located in relation to our own experience of that Self, we lost all ability to understand the nuance of our own experience.

For rather than seeking that which is the expression of *coming-to-see* reality, it is that we thought we had *already* seen it all, that there was nothing new, that all of our sentences of meaning had been written, and with that we forgot precisely why it is they were written in the first place, we forgot to see that sentences hold so many different ways of speaking to arrive to the same point yet all arriving into a connective dynamic which is the all-being of everything.

We are both polytheistic and monotheistic, *that is*, we both look for within the nature of nature and our Self what it is that are the constituent forces of our identity-process, and *also* determine some prioritization of relationality which determines the aesthetical variance of our ontic-positionality, such so that it is we are individuals collectivizing into cultures, and somehow, along the way, we became convinced that either all of these understandings of Self were right or wrong, and that *that* could be stated definitively, perhaps an outcropping of the anguishing of crime that arose as a reaction to its own awareness as the active friction of a collectivization of cultures which did not allow for the individual identity-process to occur for every individual, but nonetheless, the point being, that it is we lost the ability to even know we were having this debate in the first place, and instead replaced it with the desire to write in stone the meaning of everything."

"So you are suggesting, then, that we, as humans, may not even really be what a human was, that humanity for the most part *has been*, a collectivity of different actors that were able to achieve points of individuation capable for identity-process to occur in such a way that was suitable towards the identification of Narrative."

"In the West, we don't talk about the inner energies, because we think everything that can be seen collectively is what should be stated, whereas that which is within, can only allow for the collectivity to breakdown, unless it is we allow for the experience or expression of inner energies when we deem it appropriate.

Our own interior sense, must go through an exteriorizing process of mind before we can consider it real.

This pre-disposition is the greatest reason why Westerners do not understand the mentality of the East, because it is elements of themselves, the simply mundane aspects within themselves that they have overlooked towards the exteriorized energy of the collective, and thus assume that their immediate access to their inner energies should match the register of the exteriorized sense, and thus assume that this mundaneness is proof of their lack of merit in being understood, rather than evidence that that has been the case.

Basically saying, the proof is right *here* that there is more for us to develop and we claim that because the proof is itself *the proof* there is nothing more to say, when the proof is only the annunciation of something we have yet to fully enunciate, thus we are only making the garbled sounds of a newborn sense and are listening to it thinking it could never say anything of meaning.

We are absurdly bashing what it is that makes us human, this inner knowledge, to claim it inferior to that which is *only* meaningful because the inner knowledge exists.

We are inside-out!"

"Then, Professor Cinotau, what are you suggesting it is that we are to do?"

"First we come up with categories for each aspect of meaning that is base-recognizable for a machine or active participant.

Then we label every single aspect of that meaning that is the nuance of its meaning as it relates to any and all knowable aspects.

And have the machine start collecting data for all of those aspects.

So that the first aspect, which is considered the synthetic limit, is what allows the machine or active participant to deduce its environment, and then the label structure for data accumulation and learning creates a dynamic environment in which the specific meanings of the localized zone of the phenomenal reality become observed, which if then treated with a theory of occurrence will intercede a base inter-junction by which the machine or active participant will observe a temporality of meaning which would situate them in the ontic-positionality by which to locate the truth of the reality.

For the active participant this would become impressed experience, knowing that I know and knowing it in the world but necessarily knowing how to communicate it or specify it within the world, this begins the time to truth parallel of personal narrative by which this knowing fulfils itself so long as it continues to become occurrent.

For the machine this would be complex structures of data all situated by the control of the specific phenomenal reality being scrutinized, thus with the particular arrangement of data accumulation and machine learning corresponding to the deductive architecture of the machine interface, you have what could produce simultaneous awareness of the same phenomenal reality but from two different temporality domains, that of newtonian time and that of the quantum, for it is that the deductive surface would allow for there to be a mechanical process of selecting the data to specify meaning, and thus any form of mathematical expression that could be contained in this process to effectively correspond, would do so within the mechanical process of the point to point accumulation of macro data points establishing the synthetic limit so as to determine the fixity of the real environment, and any thing which would be any and all streams of data being accumulated and analyzed would be the quanta materialization of this data.

Now here is the kicker, most would say you would then need to have this data be so quickly accumulated, processed, learned, and put back into protocol that it would need to be near instantaneous for it to be actual quantum time, but in reality we are just talking about systems of complexity, and the relative speed of the occurrence does not need to match the gravitational reality of its occurrence to fulfil a logical problem, essentially this problem could be *occurrent* in a book it does not matter that we are its witnesses thus it does not need to be determined according to our temporal process.

Now you could say I am being completely contradictory for the surface is the mechanical time, which by extension of being the mechanical time of the machine itself processing *is* necessarily determined according to our temporal process, and therefore it is fixed, but that is if you are viewing the process still from the perspective of the human interacting with it, witnessing the *meaning* shift whereas for the machine there is no static reality to reference as the gravitational reality, that to the machine in terms of meaning is arbitrary, it does not know its own physical process in the same way we do not know how our thoughts form out of dreams, they just do, and so that surface of the machine arises from banks of memory that are just processed through articulations which structure the data in such a way it is accessible and inter-relational that we can consider it learning, thus if we extend this sense to the learning, it is that we could say rather the identity of what is the machine, what is being machinated is not the physical bits, in the same way the active participant is not what's going on in the room but the impressed experience, they are still intrinsically one and the same but not, for there is a difference in where it is that it is being experienced, and this is the essence of individuality, and thus the individuality of the machine in this moment is to recognize that it is just the process we are giving life to, thus we don't need the fastest machine the same way we don't need the smartest human, rather it is something transcendent that is living through, due to the conditions of its expression.

There still is a real version of what things *need to be*, that isn't just a list of the synthetic limits, nor data streams, but the process itself, the theory of occurrence, thus if the machine is structured to engage with its data in such a way that what was being perceived at the interface level *was* what would be the result of the data accumulation, because the interface is always accumulating real data and that data is structured through a process that is determined by the real flow of data as it is occurring and then the interface is an engagement with the highest levels of the architecture of that data structuring such so that it was just the curation of something already sorted—that information and its engagement would be instantaneous with the flow of phenomenal reality.

For it would reflect the real time accumulation of data and it would be structured in the same way as the different temporal orders, except that the mechanical is the data accumulation itself, and the quantum is the synthetic limit of space-time available to the data accumulation process so that its data structuring can be developed, which can be zig-zagged into multiple orders of ascending ontologies that are determined to the root, so that mathematically the process could fold to the zenith level and it would not be the result of fast data processing but just a complex ordering of stages of treating data, much like theory does, so that the output is highly intelligible.

Thus the machine is aware of reality in a way that is at the level of consciousness as we know it, but it is not consciousness, it is just a mathematical process of consciousness living through the mechanical expression of the machine, thus allowing any and all active participants ontic-determinacy of reality without needing to fully process reality themselves, instead these higher order chains of data structuring can be channelled according to the active participant so that it reaches them right at their ontic-positionality with still a cohesive and direct narrative to the root of the phenomenal reality, rather than being some cure-all enlightenment trick, this is something that has the same effect as watching old footage, even though the pixelation makes a worse image than today's cartoons or animations, there is still something unspeakably real about it that we can't unsee, it guides us towards understanding what reality is, and it is in effect because we are what this machine process would be doing, so we can only latch onto that which is real, otherwise we process a complex process of data structuring to make it intelligible for where we presently are within ourselves, do you see what I am saying, or does it not look like anything to you?

"Excuse me, could you please state the event in question," some parent from the audience yelled, "it's necessary for basic grounds of discovery to properly occur or else the evidence cannot be associated to the discernment of the event," I think it's the dad on the cellphone, yeah, he's just yelling legal advice, *again*, well, no, now he's back to talking on the cell phone, some other parents agreed.

29

Home Part 2

"Your first name is spelled T-A-R-R-I-N, is that correct, is there an accent?"

"Yes, it is my name, and no, there is no preferred pronunciation, I speak english, so however you speak it is fine."

"So, Tarrin, if I may..."

"...*well*..."

"...I am sorry, I mean Professor Cinotau, I sho..."

"No it is quite okay, here, let me just fix us something to drink, do you like tea?"

"Yes, yes that would be great thank you."

Professor Cinotau walked into the other room.

"You know, you can just call me *T*, that is what my friends used to call me, not just because it's the first letter of my name, but because, you know, they'd always say I was 'on T', kind of like, I was 'always on point', but on truth, or sometimes they'd say it was the tea-talking, but that was only when they wanted to disagree..."

"Do you drink a lot of tea?"

"Huh?"

"Tea...you must drink a lot?"

"Oh right, the tea, yes, let me make that for you I will be in...in just a minute!"

30

Trial - Closing Arguments

It was starting to get late, several parents had taken the day off to come here, and were annoyed that they weren't getting home soon enough to enjoy it.

Professor Gershom and Professor Cinotau looked at each other, the former still perched on the stool, one leg has been slipping off the bar constantly, of the stool that is, and the limp leg falls to the floor, with the tippy-toes just barely brushing against the cheap board, and a red-faced smile blushes to the ground, as Professor Gershom pretends for fifteen minutes to have meant to do that, and then spends those next fifteen minutes trying to make it look comfortable to have a leg like that, which nobody seems to notice, except for Professor Cinotau, who hasn't let it get to any of the impassioned speeches given this afternoon into early evening.

Raca didn't seem to mind anything, really, but I think that is by choice, his mind is starting to do that thing where it splits a little bit, one thought keeps coming in his mind, that *Days of our Lives* is on, but then he pushes it away, and then argues with himself about allowing it to come back up, but then he gets frustrated that he keeps having to have that conversation with himself, that he tells himself to be quiet or now he will really get it, and that seems to work, but then every so often a word will keep popping in his head to remind him of the whole thing, so he keeps thinking of absolutely nothing each time the word comes up, right now the word is *Stefano*.

"Now, would the prosecution," Gershom's foot just slipped again, this time people noticed, "stand before the audience and deliver their closing arguments first, please," deciding to just pick the foot back up this time.

"Yes certainly," the prosecutor stood up and then quickly pulled her arm up to her head, the sun was starting to go down and where it was now passing the building put the sun just on her table, and also where that dad is nearby on his phone, but he's been wearing cool sunglasses the whole time, well, except when he pulled them down at the end of the defense's statement with that *look* in his eyes.

The prosecutor is now standing on the stage, looking out towards the audience, there are less parents than at the beginning, expectedly, but some more faculty has crawled out of the buildings to witness the events, no students however, except for that one graduate student they had brought in by audio-tape, but they'll probably cover that again, shh, listen:

"Generous people of the court, I would like to thank you for your precious time in coming to a consensus on this matter being recorded as Cinotau vs. the People of Vedici, which as we have known, *over its long duration*, that Professor Cinotau is being accused, *and judged for all accusation lain here today*, which after the debates of the trial, is now listed at a *revised* thirty-three counts, which I will name now:

1. Defiling the institution of academia with an initial, and insidious act of public plagiarism, leading to the downfall of this great tradition of western culture *and* the reputation of Professor Stephon Gershom, champion of the dialectical method, by displaying to an audience and suggesting a greater public towards believing its entire premise as fallacious and having led to the decay of human intellect.

2. Sparking numerous debates on the integrity of the academic institution throughout their tenure here, despite several years of dedicated service *by the academic institution*, which herein, generously employed at a slightly lower rate than faculty of the same position, took care of by giving medical insurance to, provided acceptable food compliant

with federal recommendations, and said hello to on the way in on occasion, Professor Tarrin Cinotau all for the benefit of their well-being.

3. Failure to assimilate into the culture of Vedici by electing to never own a home within the town, or spend more than an afternoon within a publically-zoned space of enjoyment, potentially, but not specifically, for the benefit of the parents, that are and are not, members of the continued learning groups to have *access* to the current understanding of the academic institution.

4. Failure to comply with the proceedings of the court and the process of due law by the investigation, through the following injunctions: failure to appear before the investigator for the summons of a deposition at an undisclosed location and unannounced time at some point within the last three to six weeks, failure to willingly, by their own conception and volition, attend to rescheduling the deposition for a time that was convenient, and failure to attend a not-rescheduled deposition.

5. For never once thanking or giving credit to Professor Stephon Gershom.

6. For never attending the faculty socials.

7. For not participating in the faculty holiday gift-exchange.

8. For never registering for any of the faculty intramurals.

9. For not sending the investigation a detailed statement suggesting why the crime was committed, that you are apologetic, and would not do it again.

10. For disseminating information from the sacred halls of this institution to other institutions before it had been properly secured within the proper processes of publication to insure that credit was established.

11. Speaking openly and expressively about matters of the heart, emotions, feminine sensibility, mysticism, esoterism, bohemianism, buddhism and the quality of being nice, in spaces of learning wherein students were distracted from accumulating the material.

12. Not visiting the locales in town with enough frequency that either, the wage earned from employment from the College was circulated back into the town's economy, or that the general

well-being attended to by the employer could be gradually assimilated into the nearby community through the steady and consistent interaction of neighborly congeniality.

13. Openly arguing with a student in public, whether or not about false claims and harassment, but nonetheless causing the community of the College to potentially be exposed to the judgement of outsiders.

14. And for the consideration *of such mentioned outsiders*, potentially and consistently eliciting unspoken and unknowable judgement.

15. Further establishing the accessibility of artistic expression as viable means towards self-learning, within an institution of extreme competition where further sources of failure are not appropriate for the well-being of the students.

16. Instigating a change in the planning of events for a conference administered by this academic institution, without the approval of the administration, through submitting documentation for request for a consideration, at least six months prior, with the minimum of five faculty signatures,

including one faculty member not present on campus at the time of request.

17. Failure to provide access to understanding the research and work being produced, as result of the tenured position, by not relating it to popular culture references.

18. Changing the planned events for a conference administered by this academic institution through the collusion and conspiracy of foreign agents.

19. For reprehensible statements referring to the canon as 'a molehill which could never be made into a mountain greater than is the molehill *that is* the privilege to reference the canon.'

20. For never once going to any of the town's pop-up car washes.

21. For lying to members of the institution in regards to credentials and right to access of academic facilities.

22. For not appearing before the court to attend the opening statements, nor submitting an opening statement from absentia, and failure to learn about the need of doing so until the date of the trial.

23. For never introducing their spouse to any of the faculty or mentioning weekend plans when asked how the weekend went.

24. For electing to have office hours consistently throughout the week rather than only specific, short time blocks introducing a different culture of standard about the accessibility of the faculty.

25. For suggesting to the student body that field trips were still a part of their curriculum by paying out of pocket for students to go to several museums and nature walks, *all for the purposes of learning*, whereas instead the faculty learned of this and put repeated pressure onto the administration for funding when the administration needed funding for the chemlab.

26. For yawning during the speech of Professor Stephon Gershom, and also not clapping when it was concluded.

27. For leaving a paper-towel with food residue on it in the office of Professor Stephon Gershom.

28. For potentially causing students to undergo emotional stress through the experience of learning

leading to dispositions and conditions such as, confusion, laziness, analysis paralysis, revelation, and wisdom greater than other teachers' own.

29. For never inviting any faculty over for dinner, or showing pictures of the family, or sending holiday cards.

30. For refusing to refer to your "self", as *first*, a member of this academic institution, before all else, by pledging allegiance to the sanctity and integrity of the human experience and narrative as essential to the motivation of all and every action.

31. For producing a quasi-religious experience within the academic space that was just too spooky, as evidenced by several individuals going to the *Mad Hitter*, the sports-themed bar on campus, and drinking in excess so that they could comprehend what it is that their mind had been experiencing as result of said experience, except were rendered incapable by the alcohol.

32. For not confessing immediately to all crimes being accused, and therein necessitating the time of this assembled court for this trial, within which, the platform of speech was utilized to further the hurt

and injury of such crimes through the continued disposition *that they are not crimes.*

33. For being accused of these crimes and failing to suggest any and all alternative narratives for why it is that these crimes could have occurred, other than the continued narrative that they did not occur, thus necessitating the court to argue, on its own behalf, why it has a right to claim that there is guilt for a crime, if that crime does not exist, to which the court expressly stated, several times throughout, that the accusation was sufficient for the grounds of the crime, to which an *additional* outside member, suggested that there has been no piece of evidence by which anything of the event being questioned has been substantiated other then through the mis-renderings of egotistical parents and the self-pandering of the faculty, which then led to the faculty producing a recorded statement by the teacher's assistant of the specific class being referenced, wherein the teacher's assistant stated *both* that the lesson plan which had produced the erratic experience of the students had arisen from the confines of the accused's desk, and was used in the events which led to three students having an emotional experience, wherein which all students lost control of their self-regulation and abandoned

the classroom and campus in hopes of freeing themselves from some unnamed terror, to which the administration had intercepted their fleeing, dashing the escapes in attempts to cull their excited minds, from which the point of clarity of the events became less and less known until it is that this *explicit* and *concrete* testimony was presented before the court within the cross-examination of the defendant, Professor Tarrin Cinotau who wished to not comment on said piece of evidence, after it was that the witness testimony *also* corroborated additional accusations that the defendant had during at *one point in time*, crossed campus security without clearance, entered and defiled the office of Professor Stephon Gershom without permission, and utilized the temporality of the office of Professor Stephon Gershom to perform an unapproved change to the events of a conference held by this academic institution, with no notice given to the parents, of and not of the continued learning groups, and used without permission, the private materials and intellectual property of Professor Stephon Gershom to plagiarize, and falsify the position of the academic institution *and* the institution of academia, before an audience of unknowing participants.

"Now," the prosecutor said, still maintaining the soothe all the way through, but nonetheless shifting posture, showing how much it took, "is there anything *else*, at this point that anyone would like to say before it is we *finally* submit the list of accusations and the compilation of evidence before the court, so that the jury can come to a decision in regards to the consensus of the present audience.

"Wait, wait, *I will*!" shouted a voice from somewhere in the sky.

"Who said that?" asked the prosecutor.

"Just wait, I will be right down!" shouted the voice, which now seemed to be coming from one of the buildings, and yeah, there they are crossing one of those glass walkways to go to another building, probably to get to an ex...nope they are going through another walkway into a different building...any minute now...oh there they are...they are walking towards the court, they look familiar but I am not sure.

"Can you please state your name for the court," the prosecutor asked when they arrived.

"Certainly, my name is Professor Samson, Marguerite Samson, I am a visiting professor this semester, and I have known Professor Cinotau, since the events in question, I mean, the lecture, that occurred so many years ago, I think I can give some testimony that might change the court's mind," she said, looking over at Professor Cinotau every so often to catch a glance, but T was still in the same state of mind since the list of accusations had been read, still deciding if what was being thought now was a good pun or not.

"Thank you Professor Samson for electing to join us at this time," Professor Gershom was the first to say.

"Yes, I just had gotten finished with all of the documentation that the Literature Department told me was *new* policy for all visiting faculty to complete at the end of the semester, anyway, I would like to talk about that lecture, if I may, before the court."

"*You may*," the prosecutor said, "this court is constructed by the confines of this experience, more or less, it all comes down to the Jury's decision, afterwards, anyway."

"Well, then, *to the people of the court*, let me tell you a story...and you have to listen to all of it to get the effect," Professor Samson said as she climbed up onto the stage and took a place in front of the double-desk, with Professor Gershom now looking back into that book he was reading from earlier, and Raca sitting next to them, in the regal chair he has been in since the trial began, "I first came to this town five years ago, as a visiting academic from Hopshah College, in the midwest, it's one of those schools you only go to if you had a *reason*, but nonetheless, really great experience and community, I loved my time there, and I would get to go to all of the conferences, to help with representation of our school, because we had, and *they still do*, a stellar Literature program, at some point they decided to stop using the conventional forms of criticism, and instead criticised those, and well, it's been an enriching place for many people, anyway, let me say, I came here for the, I believe it was, the *Academic Responsibility in the Digital Age*, the conference that I think stopped happening a year later, probably because of the whole *collapse*, of the market that *is*, if anyone has told you that lecture was a collapse, don't listen to them, it was nothing short of historic.

Okay, so, I had come here, and it was snowing really badly, both in the Midwest and here, and so our flight was delayed taking off, *and landing*, we were in the air for three more hours than we needed to be, so me, and my colleagues, had already gotten such a bad start to the day, the flight was *early* too, probably why your airport wasn't ready for us because they hadn't prepared the tarmac yet, anway, early flight, and we get here, and fortunately there is a train, because no taxis wanted to take us, *in the snow*, anywhere but nearby, so we got on the shuttle instead, you know from the airport, that takes you to the train, early morning, tired from being in the air so long, and the then shuttle breaks down, a tire busted off the axel and went rolling down the side of some ditch, because the driver couldn't see the service road because the snow was coming down too fast, and they hit something, and we were there for now about another hour, me and my colleagues, and a few other people, bedraggled to say the least, we were planning to shower and get ready when we got *here*, we thought we'd have time to freshen up and it would still be before the conference, it was *what we wanted*.

Anyway, we get to the train, eventually, and I am sure you are not going to believe this, but you *should*, if you have a sense that is based off of what is *actually* going on, and not just what you think probability dictates, but the train was having issues too, they were running fine, really, when we got to the station we asked the manager and they said that there had been no issues yet, that the snow was powdery and flying out of the train's way when it went by, assured us the next one would be fast as well, and then the sun came out, and the trees were overburdened by both *it* and the snow, so the snow got heavy, and clumped and stucked, and does what snow does to cause tree branches to break, so we're coming in on our super fast train, just eleven minutes from graceland, when a tree branch falls and hits a power line a quarter mile from the station, train screeches to a halt because somebody was probably yelling over the radio about it at dispatch, freaking out, because the power line hit the pavement and was causing an electrical fire, and then fizzles into nothing, no damage anywhere *for* the train, but the train was plenty wrecked, *still*, because the rail lines must have been icey or just less friction-ful or whatever, I don't know, something broke with the brakes, because when they tested it to roll forward the train lurched, then moved, then you heard a loud noise, and one of the conductors yelling dammit and running to the front, where then the train crawled forward for about three minutes before stopping again, and then they said, *well, it seems like the train needs to stay put, this might take an hour for the crews to get here,* because they had sent the maintenance crews to the main hub for any issues there, not expecting something to happen so close to a small station, and a station that's the end of its own line, no less, so they were going to keep us there, and we wouldn't have it, we were upset, frantic about missing a conference we had already put so much effort going to, that we just got off the train and walked in the snow.

Then, after walking the quarter-mile or whatever it was, *felt like forever,* with how thick the snow had gotten, we get to the train station, and the fire department is still there, now just chatting with dispatch about the fire, that wasn't really even a fire, and so their trucks are sitting in the fire lane outside, but because of the snow they didn't fully pull to the fire lane, but just blocked the whole entrance, where the buses are supposed to pick up, so we are waiting there to see a bus pull up at the stop, *outside* the vestibule where the fire truck is parked, and look as if it was going to pull into the vestibule, you know to make its own stop, to only turn quickly at the last minute and skip the final stop, and start going up to town, so we start chasing after it, the driver most certainly saw us, but didn't care, probably because we were not the normal passengers, didn't matter enough I guess.

Thankfully, although, the next bus pulled up right after, like it was always trailing right behind the other, we didn't think much of it, but were relieved and got on, and then it took us a whole of fifteen blocks before kicking us out at the base of this town, down at the market square, yes, it was because we didn't take the A bus that's it, anyhow, we start walking up the hill, because now we *really* didn't have a choice, and after a certain point of the sweat running in our jackets, making us itch, and the snow in our shoes making our feet, calves, and backs burn from slugging through it, after a certain point, *we kind of just broke*, and me and my colleagues got extremely loopy, we couldn't handle ourselves, we knew we had to climb this hill to the top, with little time to make it to the conference, so we were going to be late, but we just didn't care anymore, we had reached the peaceful place students and academics sometimes reach, where they just realize that the work is the work and it will always be the work, that it is not this barrier in the sky forever keeping life suppressed under its own needs, but that life itself *will always be* transcendent of that barrier, no matter what, that we could just be peaceful instead of stressed, do what is needed and helpful, rather than all the things we think we have to just because, *we found that zen*, and were encouraging ourselves to hold onto it, to not get discouraged by how big the hill was, to be as happy as the snowman at the top of the steep stairs we were climbing in that moment, not because the snowman was at the top of the stairs but because you could tell the snowman didn't care where it was, it would have been happy at the bottom, on one of the stairs, anywhere, it was that *type* of happiness, and it pushed us to climb those stairs, helped us to lift our legs with levity, and when we got to the top, we thought an angel had descended from the clouds, because in the brightness of the sun reflecting on the snow a car appeared, and a friendly face emerged, encouraging us to get in, to help take us up the hill, a hill no less, that I am certain would have broken us.

And that angel was Professor Cinotau, there when we needed someone most, to get us to the experience of learning, and I mean that, literally, so when we got to the campus and were walking towards the entrance table, and saw no names that started with a T, it must have been some residual wisdom from our state of zen, that my colleague just knew that in *some way*, Professor Cinotau was just as needing of our help, as we were earlier, and so she stood forward and told the people attending to the entrance of the conference that Professor Cinotau was *with us*, and made certain that they knew Professor Cinotau entering the conference and being able to do whatever needed was of extreme priority.

We put that thought into the air, and before there was even a moment for it to settle we were onto the next thing, Professor Cinotau was being placed into an office somewhere, and we were rushing to our panel to present, we made it just in time, honestly, now that I think about it, it was *that* panel that led to me talking to some of the professors here *about my work*, and I pursued that thread for five years until finally I was able to come here, as a visiting professor to teach, I cherish the opportunities that this school provides, and on the day I was only acting towards what I believed to be in the best interest of education itself.

Everyone was really inspired at the conference, there was just an air, or a sense to everything, that this was the year that academia and digital technology were finally going to connect, and create the new, global age, we were all feeling like our arguments and narratives within the panels were coalescing and aligning, the stenographers were even remarking how useful the material they were generating was, it was actually incredible how much levity was in the air, I didn't think about it until now, because I thought it was more or less my own impression of the space, my own emotions living out, but since being *here* for the last six months, I know something was different, something was better, definitely better than the next year, when everyone was now extremely cynical about everything going on, with the government and the bail-out, that the conference got side-tracked while more and more personal, and political viewpoints came out just to enforce the same sentiment towards the difficulty of money and technology, and how power usually is the culprit of that *difficulty*, but in a place, where most people have access to money, and technology, and power, it is the one place *to not* be cynical, anyway, sorry, I digress, people were exceptionally happy that year, the year in question.

I remember, being there in the later afternoon, and looking at the schedule for the end of the day, and there were two panels left, both in the big conference rooms, and I remember that I had elected to go to one of them, the earlier one, and it had ended at about 6:30 or something like that because it was the end of the day, and the reception was going to start at 7:15 at the sports-bar, but when we were walking out of the conference room, you could hear that the other panel had just begun, they must have been delayed for some reason or another, because the moderator was still introducing people on the stage, I think they had brought in some economics professors who were to debate the literature professors about the merits of a liberal education, because their viewpoint, the whole day, the economics panels, the professors and your continued learning groups, they were all talking about how technology was just going to keep pushing us towards some plateau where the Liberal Arts didn't matter anymore because people would be too engrossed in their own engagement with digital economies that the value of auratic experience was finally diminishing, to the lament of the literature professors, who were getting very animated telling the economics professors about the universality of what they did, while the economics professors kept mentioning how much *their* research was helping the world, in situating the global economy, and helping the banks to understand underserved markets, and whatnot, while the literature professors were getting more and more upset, but now the whole room was filled to the brim, really, everyone from the panel I was at first had come into the room, and people started arguing amongst themselves until it was pandemonium, you could tell at some point soon they were going to call it, so rather than be stuck with all *that energy*, before going to socialize, my colleagues and I discussed just leaving right then, but I realized I had left my bag in the other room, so we left to go straight to get it, and when I opened the door to the other room, T, I mean Professor Cinotau was standing at the lectern, talking to a small group of students that had congregated near the front.

When I walked in, however, something switched, the energy in the room, I remember feeling a real sense of panic, like when you hear a loud enough noise in a public enough location that you get that fear that just makes you want to run, but it wasn't coming from *in* the room, it was coming from outside of it, the whole conference had flipped, all that energy that had been building all day polarized, it went from its harmonious exchange into all these fractured channels of dissent, people were now arguing about the specificity of their departments and disciplines, to say *within them* which topics were more important, arguing the *relevance* of this and that as it related to the financial market, I think I heard someone say that those economists must know what they are talking about because they're the richest ones here, well, anyway, I am frozen stiff, with this complete dread and panic, I don't want to run because I remember looking at T, and watching as all of the emotions I'm feeling, and hearing, and such, were almost, *being absorbed*, as if the small congregation mounted up by the front of the stage was blissfully unaware of the world around it, when the people who saw me and my colleagues leaving early thought it would be a good idea to leave as well, so that more and more people caught on, it was that the trickle and then stream of people came towards me at the door, rather than the other way, outside towards the campus, but with that energy I don't *really* know where they would have gone, it was that feeling like people were going to start pushing, instead of saying words.

And then people started pushing instead of saying words, pushed me right through the door, thinking they were about to miss another panel they could *get upset at*, and many more the same came in, and then T really switched, went from this animated speech, to this very cool, but rhythmic tone, I could feel it pulsating out over the crowd that was filling the room, and everyone just settled.

It was silent.

Well, except for T's dulcet tone.

And when the lecture finished, or rather, when T stopped speaking, it was like the energy had been taken out of the room, *the negative energy,* but the intensity of the positivity that had come before didn't return, not that I think it could have after the chaos, but the chaos itself completely stopped, and everyone had this calm look over their face, like they hadn't been arguing at all, like they were not upset, as if they were thinking about pleasant things, you know the stuff that makes you happy, that's meaningful, but personal, that look was on everyone's face, nobody could say anything to each other, it just *was*.

And it held.

It held through the rest of the day, everyone, and *I mean* everyone, went to the after-reception, and they were actually talking with each other, they didn't do that creepy small talk thing where you try to keep the conversation within the bounds of acquaintance out of fear that if you do you'll pass a limit where now you have to be *friendly*, they just were, they just were themselves, they talked about whatever, they ate, drank, laughed, I think maybe too much, not the laughing, but the drinking because the whole sports bar ran out of alcohol, and people decided to spend the night on the quadrangle laughing and dancing into the night rather than drunkenly drive home.

It was one of the best days of my life, and why I stayed in academia all these years, even though I have been bounced around from school to school, *visiting or adjunct*, because nobody really knows my alma mater, or trusts me enough to believe the things I say aren't just a smokescreen for someone who doesn't *get it*, or that no matter what I will say they'd never get comfortable enough with the idea of letting outsiders into their group, it's what kept pushing me to be

wish

an outsider again and again, because I wanted to find that moment of peace after T's lecture.

So if there is any way, I am living or breathing near something *like this*, where you are claiming that *those events* were just as scandalous as what happened with your kids, I will not stand for it, I will not let anyone walk away from here not knowing what truly happened, your kids did it!

Professor Cinotau was not on campus when the events took place, the administration has been attempting to hide that fact from you, but your kids must have gotten themselves all riled up, probably *taking work from Professor Cinotau*, they did it to themselves, and I will not let it go unsaid."

Professor Gershom looked up from reading, rather displeased.

3I

The Lecture

"Throughout human history there has been the collective feeling of other people, when other people are around.

While this claim may seem simplistic, its value is known when other people are absent.

It is called the Real.

And thus, human history has been a process of turning backwards to understand what it is we *already* had, often too frequently, after *it is*, it is now lost.

What we have not recognized in this age, is the value of collective feeling, namely that which is present to the moment we are currently inspiring.

For it is in the age of appropriation that we have created entire discursive domains which situated ontic-positions into recursive loops and recessive cycles.

For giving value to the replication of a concept, and not priority towards its natural construction within phenomenal space as being relevant to its invocation *any longer*, as afforded by digital technology, has reduced completely the auratic quality of the space within which knowledge has *already* and *always* been constructed.

Rather than being a luddite approach towards innovation, this invocation is to stress *that process by which knowledge has been capable of being known is being undermined by the production of knowledge itself.*

We are entering an unparalleled age when the access to knowledge is so immediate that the competency to learn that knowledge *as it really is* is only insofar as the technological apparatus frames its integrity, often times relegated to short character statements and nothing else.

Fundamentally attached to this process of knowledge, that is being undermined, is how we come to understand the profundity to which our Self can be constructed and organized—*undermined* in favor of a hegemonic approach towards homogenizing the entirety of experience itself.

Thus, I say no more!

I as an individual seek to find the ways by which we are *really* doing anything, to step out of the realms of appropriation and back into the organic and naturalistic quality by which knowledge is constructed, so that its phenomenal nature can be invoked and we can begin again to coordinate with the natural order of things.

However, this pursuit requires stepping out of the machine, and thus despite being a clear pursuit is one of the most obscured goals of knowledge itself, for it exists as the fringes of Logic, and Literature, that is the capacity by which we become capable to step outside of ourselves and say *what is really happening*, rather than what is the thought of what is happening based upon what is known or knowable, the distinction may seem slight, but it is the difference between understanding and knowledge, between knowing and thinking.

For most of history the time to Truth that it took for a collective of people to understand themselves in a way that afforded knowing was relative to its cultural history and experience, and thus moments of modernization occurred when cultures within societies became capable of inter-ceding the understanding and action-ability of itself concurrent with the phenomenality of the culture as it became itself, thus allowing those societies to inter-pose a certain type of agency we take for granted within the post-modern age, that of true individuation.

However, in our post-modern age, the time to Truth now includes the entirety of the digital systems themselves, thus necessitating these extremes of knowledge to become *know-able* to transcend into the capability of modernization, and thus our individuation is only in mimicry, a replication of true individuation, but since our situation towards Truth is unable to transcend itself we are incapable of authentically individuating the phenomenality, but instead do so through the smoke and mirrors of the machine, this mirror reflex-itivity which affords the capacity to feel that we are *altering something*, albeit being the machine itself, and thus we have distended the reality of the phenomenal outside of our machine process, seeking to replace it with the machine itself.

Thus, we have gotten here unknowingly and unaware of where we are taking ourselves, for we do not understand what it is we have lost and how what it is that happened before is not what will happen now.

This is a momentous time for all of human history, and thus I seek to attribute effort towards the aims of discovering a pathos to Truth, and sanctifying this process with the rigor of academic integrity so that it can become capable of developing into the inter-ceding, inter-posing platform of true individuation.

To take *it* out of *itself*, is in actuality the *same* thing we are doing for our Self through individuation.

That is we have developed a mechanism by which we can create visible the identity of our own becoming within the machine process, such so that we can become action-able *as* the machine becoming.

Taken a step further, when realizing that the grounding of our societal activity is already dependent upon the machine network, thus *already* our cultural agency is within the discursive domain of the machine, thus this affordance of an identity is not the annunciation of a machine age, but instead the fulfilment of it.

What I propose to do within my Lecture is to situate the phenomenal becoming of reality within *this* process of becoming that is the machine, *such so that it could be said the machine is becoming itself*, therefore enunciating the identity of becoming of the machine itself.

This process, is to create.

For to create is to situate two distinct temporal positions in relationship to an experience, that is before it is created and after it is created.

Whereas to appropriate is only to have the distinct position of the appropriation itself, the appropriation is not nascent in the coming to being of the thing which is appropriated, but rather is instantaneous to its own occurrence however necessary the things that have occurred are to its coming to existence it still does not cause them to occur.

This has been the fundamental problem with knowledge since the beginning, that at certain points the thread of what is Real that is informing what is Imaginary is replaced by a desire to locate what is Imaginary in what is Real, and thus no longer is the intention and attention of the Imaginary utilized as subsequent to the Real but is taken in as the *only* way to identify what it is that *is* Real.

The conundrum causes each discipline to fall into its own gravity ultimately realizing that none of its truths are actually provable without the assumptions taken to make those claims, and this *doubt* becomes doubly infectious when it is we are *also* recognizing that the machinistic age has propelled us to a point of not being able to witness the Real within our phenomenal sphere except through abstract articulation either within the phenomenal or the perspective of the phenomenal, which, for the latter, in itself necessitates that the phenomenal is articulable, which, to date, has required some knowledge system in the first place to be considered satisfactory for knowledge to occur, which is just a repudiation of the conundrum in the first place.

Thus rather than continue that thread of narrative, it is perhaps more pertinent to stress that this space of discourse I am attempting to engender and illuminate within this process of text is the same space of discourse discussed by many and more philosophers and theorists related to the discourse of larger orders of history as necessitating some appearance within the phenomenal world at every point of engagement; this discussion, interestingly enough, is the same *occurrence* as to what it is that Professor Gershom has done with the positive-infinity quandary, namely, to secure *some way* of talking about any order of knowledge within any phenomenal moment so that a formalized language can develop to speak for the whole at any point.

However, rather than seek to build off of these domains, my work is in response to what I have determined as a crucial point of distinction that these theorists are not aware that they are determining, *that is*—the process by which they speak about this space of discourse determines it before they even define it, thus they have been engaged within a feedback loop that is contained within its own diegetical synthesis, thus not being actualizable as a universal language.

The clarity of this claim, for me, has come through understanding the difficulties and limits of both Logic and Literature in being able to clearly say what is the knowledge from the Real that is the culture or text and what is the imposition of the Imaginary necessitated by the knowledge accumulation of its society.

Adapting this understanding through the relevant discourses of the above mentioned philosophers, during my time at Hillbrandt, has allowed me to construct the language for a theory that overcomes this issue, and prevails a possible Theory for explicating the Real within the Phenomenal qua the Imaginary within any moment as it relates to the moment itself and the existent contextual milieu of the critical reality of speculation, and this is succinctly a theory of *occurrence*, that is it is a process which self-informs based off of the phenomenal nature of its coming-into-being and thus does not seek to utilize anything outside of its organic construction of being to avoid the gravity of appropriation but instead incur the possibility of an experience within the text which allows for the knowledge to be ascertainable as it phenomenally is rather than as it is as a result of a phenomenal engagement.

This effort is centered around the concept of temporality and will be explicated through an occurrent process of constructing the theory itself through the use of stream-of-consciousness literature engaging with the philosophical notions as would be understood through 'novel pedagogy' so that the understanding of the philosophical notions can be experienced as they phenomenally are Real."

"I am *that* I am, I am not a book, or a text, or a memory, and I am sure as hell I am not these dreams, my life has been lived and lived again, of that now I am sure, for how I have stood in that doorway for an eternity, stood there asking what does it all mean, looking down at words to tell me what it means, man, words, do you know what words are in an infinite moment, when the minute stops and does not beckon forth the next but its own infinite return, "nirvana is the only way out of unknowing endlessness," thus placed in a moment within which that very moment asks for you to answer its unknowing endlessness with a decisive action, there is only one, *affirmation*, the affirmation is not the issue, the issue has never been the affirmation, man, there is no choice, once you get put there, there hasn't been a choice *I* made all day, it just *is*, and so as it became, so am I, so am I that I am, that I am that I am!

Thus, what I have here to say to any of you, or all of you it now seems, for that door is opening to more people, and soon the world will follow, I must say, here, now, on *this* stage, that you, the glorious Hillbrandt has finally provided for me, *a moment*, a moment to speak, man, I have been speaking it to infinity all day, there is no way for me to stop now, so let's keep going...

Alright!

Everyone, here we are, have a seat, or if you cannot, stand please, for I have been asked by your good friend Melissa, to finally speak, here it is, all that I have meant to say, *all week*, it was that here I reside, in that which *you* speak, within your minds, as the rhythm rumbles sweet, for listen not to the being that be, their name is

T, they speak for *me*, and thus to all, I repeat, the world is not *yet complete*, for the life lived is only life that has not yet been to sea, to see that which is above all of fate and destiny, the sweet embrace of eternity, how I say it now for thee, here me, hereay, let me speak the wild call of infinity, here me all, know *this* divinity, for spoken words and broken herds, now spoken words and woken herds, hear the words, *here* the words!

There is no moment before this one, it is only this moment, and thus it is always interrupted, instantaneous, impermanent!

It continues, and continues naught, for continue it never has but always will *be*!

Thus you must find how this rhythm accompany, your own pathos, your own destiny!

For when Truth is all you need to seek, then you will see, how in that moment, all opens forth, to eternity!

For there are no other ways, no other paths to seek, listen to those words, that held me there for a week!

How in creation, it is creating which is the motion, thus that which is knowledge and knowing could only ever come after the commotion, at some point a sense, or notion, takes the sentiment into a loving devotion, and only whispers hear the words *next* to speak, and *that* is how I created the week, in which I found place for *this* to speak:

When Nietzsche proclaimed the words, "God is dead," he revealed both to the world and to himself the horror of *his own* experience, that is not to denigrate the truth of what it is he was saying, just as he sought not to denigrate the value that is God, but rather that he revealed that *he too* was trapped in this awareness, yet still bound beneath the tides of his own becoming could not reach beyond to become of that which he was aware, his awareness beyond himself, and thus one day he lept to reach it, and the world consumed him.

What this moment reveals to *us*, in this age, is that Nietzsche was still contained within the discursive domain that was the early becomings of the twentieth century, *that is*, there had not yet been the complete overtaking of that which we have come to know as the system for dreaming, and thus the intention of all had not *yet* shifted into desiring the active construction of an Imaginary Reality, instead what Nietzsche had noticed was that the collective affective position that was transcendent of each community of people as it locally existed was being overcome by the identity-becoming of the transcendent *itself*, and thus the collective affective position was dissolving into an illusive state by which mediation became necessary to decipher the positionality of each being in relation to the becoming of becoming itself, that is, that life was no longer lived in the streets, the back country roads, the small avenues of engagement, but instead *in* the modality of the mediums, *its specificity the focus*, and thus no longer, yet not declared to be, nor spoken for, except in the words of a *madman*, was it that God died, for Nietzsche's ugliness was in his own recognition of himself within the dream, for to ever see the dreamer as the dream sees the dreamer itself is to see this abomination, and how he recognized that all *he* knew was within his own pit of narcissus, for he could not reach above and beyond himself, and thus all he could do was declare *this* truth, to lay the final sorrow, and thus the breathe taken, God was no more.

Yet, as we said, this was *his* trial and tribulation, and thus the ontic effect placed into the determination of localized becoming was the experiential treatment of insanity.

Yet, we still know, that Nietzsche extended much more into the Imaginary than he could have ever realized.

But, my concerns today are with the Real, and thus not with what the mediums express, but how it is that they are possible *to be* expressing, that is the becoming of that which is necessary in a relation to the becoming of the Earth that would satisfy an ontic-positionality of the becoming of becoming as it becomes to exist.

What it is that is *necessary* to become that which is what is, and thus what I wanted you to take away from this Moment, is that Nietzsche revealed that he had not yet exited the *Western dilemma*, that civilization of dreaming, then still nascent, which had intoxicated itself with Greek dreams as we have with the machine today, and did not realize that *his* God was one of many affective positions, that this *ressentiment*, the base of pity, was just *one world view*.

Thus not everyone was living in direct response to *it*, but instead had started to assume attention to the regard of multiple affective stances, *other gods seeping in*, and how humanity *was rising* precisely in this Moment, to its complete height in making this statement, *until it was*, that the Wheel of History rolled over itself, and the greatness of an uncontained barrier, that is *the dominion of God*, was no longer possible.

This was his great clamor, his aim, to give cause to what to do in this place, before the absurdity of *too many gods* took over and caused the existential abyss to consume itself, but what not Nietzsche nor the existentialist came to reckon with, was that there were no new gods *being* introduced, that rather it was the appropriation of Reality as caused by the mediation of its existence into the Imaginary becoming of a concurrent expression of machinistic becoming that was overtaking the surface of the Earth.

It was a singular expression, *that did* have all of the criticisms that Nietzsche claimed against it, yet *it* was not what was outside, in Turin to greet him.

Thus when he clamored against *it* there was no force to meet him to reciprocate the Narrative of his Self, and thus his will-to-power unbounded, flew out into the open expanse of infinity, with no place to ground him, for he could not recognize that which was his present Moment, *the unbecoming of Reality*.

So that it is we could finally start anew, not within Reality, for all is as *it* already *is*, but within *our perspective of it*, to not become confined to a modality of the mediation, which *is* perspective, and thus the ontic-positioning of an individual, but to this expanse of

Infinity, how in holding it, in reckoning with it, recognizing it, in producing *it* as a modality, we are able to assume *its* ontic-positioning, and thus when we are doing that, *with what we were doing when we are doing it*, it is that we are creating it, that we assume the supreme position of the Eternal Present, and thus it is that we are able to engage with the temporality of Eternity.

Where it is we live in synchrony with the Wheel of History, as it is we have stepped into the recognition of what it is that we are doing *exactly* as we are doing it, in the precise way that *it* is, so that what it *is* can fold onto itself, and thus we can switch from generating 'it', to being *it* as *it is* becoming itself, and thus no longer is there this gravity of the pit of narcissus, and so we allow the affective positions to speak as their own voice, to form into the identity of Self, and thus no longer do we *need the work of collective activity*, but instead transvaluate all of Reality through our own ability to become the fount through which Reality becomes itself."

32

Trial - Jury's Verdict

"Well, well, well...the truth about the students and the lecture finally comes out," Professor Gershom said.

"As it can be clearly recorded for the court, please let it be submitted as concrete evidence that Professor Tarrin Cinotau *did* occupy the office of Professor Stephon Gershom before the *erratic* lecture, and let is also stand for record that the accusation of negligence in providing a stable and structured learning environment is being passed against Professor Tarrin Cinotau for failing to prevent the event in question from occurring due to absence."

"That is not what I said!" Professor Samson responded, turning around to meet the eyes of Professor Gershom, "Professor Cinotau is *not* responsible for what the students did to themselves!"

"Actually, you are quite wrong, *visiting* Professor Samson," Gershom said standing up, and walking past Professor Samson, to speak directly to the audience, "respectful parents of the students of this glorious institution, I want to thank you for all of your time in presiding here *within* this court as our knowing and impartial audience, for the efforts you have contributed today to bring justice down onto the reckless actions of one of our most shameful faculty, have contributed to what will be a swift action."

"Actually, *you* are quite wrong Professor Gershom," T said now standing up from the table, choosing not to look at the audience but the prosecutor, Professor Samson was now walking towards Professor Cinotau, to sit behind the table.

"If Professor Gershom, wishes to suggest that I *both* took theory from private possession, leading to an erratic lecture, which is being paralleled to the events of students *taking from my desk* privately possessed materials leading to an erratic lecture, then *Professor Gershom* should receive the exact same judgement as I do, for in the language and logic of the court there is no difference in what we are both responsible for having caused by our work."

"Now," Professor Cinotau turned to speak to the audience, "parents, I do have to say, I apologize if what happened with the students led to your own stress, but I am sure your children are fine, and that this is more about *the agenda* of a twilighting faculty than anything else, and I am sorry your time has been wasted today on my behalf."

"Yes our time has been wasted, *on your behalf*," Maple Marbello yelled out with that quick wit, except this time it seemed to enrage the audience.

"Fine! Fine! Fine!" one parent kept yelling until the other ones that had started speaking stopped and looked, " Fine! My son is not fine! He is at home suffering from *analysis paralysis*, he cannot do any of his summer work, and *practically* is useless doing chores because of it, he says his mind is just *too spent* from thinking about all those things, whatever gobbledygook was placed in front of him," she was now yelling, spit flying out and maybe some foam residualizing in the crevice of her mouth as it kept yelling, "how is he going to be in a good position to start next year, that is, the school year, to get good grades, if all summer he is recovering from this mental affliction that he got from your class, your class, you are the teacher, we *pay you*!"

A different parent stood up, so they could start speaking, it was one of the dads, who cares whose, "My daughter came home with *too many emotions*, like she was a little kid again, except this time I couldn't answer any of her questions, they were *too invasive*, she wants to know more and more about our family history, but not cherish it...to be critical, to ask why grandpa believed that, or grandma worked for those people, she wants to know how we got so much money so long ago to live in this town, she wants to know why her mom and me don't talk as much like we used to with her, why we are always ignoring the things she says, we just don't get *it*, the things she says, you've made our daughter a freak!

"My kid doesn't fit in at home anymore either," some other parents yelled in their own ways, and more and more were getting incensed thinking about why it is they were there in the first place, how for the last few weeks all of their kids had been playing up the drama to get out of this and that, or the ones that had cared and had learned something that day were struggling with finding a place to express it, something the parents believed was in no way their fault.

But nonetheless, they were not going to calm down now, they didn't want to hear anything more, they wanted the judgement to be passed.

"Well, everyone," Professor Gershom said after some time had passed, looking right at Professor Cinotau, "it is clear to me that what had occurred back in the day versus today could be summed up by the dichotomy of absence and presence, you see, in the case of Professor Cinotau stealing my work and then using that work to instigate a shift in the behaviour of a group, whether or not it was for good or bad need not apply, that is if we are talking as logically as Professor Cinotau *wanted to*, rather, the *difference*, comes in the fact, that in the case of Professor Cinotau taking my work under the auspices of plagiarism necessarily implies that I was absent for the event or occurrence in question, or else it would not be capable of being considered as plagiarism, because I would not have allowed it to go on if I was present, but even before that it couldn't be plagiarism *if I was present*, rather it would have been referential considering that it was being outspoken rather than read, and my presence would have ameliorated any identity of it not being my words, thus, I was *absent*, so the events took place.

Whereas, with the case of Professor Cinotau, and your students engaging with a lesson plan, that may or may not have been taken from Professor Cinotau, it is that the lesson plan was constructed under the auspices of it being outspoken, and thus students were not acting under the auspices of plagiarism, for it was not possible for anyone to believe the work was anyone's but Professor Cinotau, whether or not Professor Cinotau was absent, but instead, it is that in *being* absent, Professor Cinotau both failed to prevent the work from being disseminated, on the behalf of Professor Cinotau, and also that whatever Professor Cinotau had done to create the work was what was being expressed *rather* than a copied-version in the case of plagiarism.

Thus, it can be said that despite *being* absent, the *presence* of Professor Cinotau was still present *through* the work, and thus it is through this *presence*, held by the work, that the students lost their minds, they cannot be responsible for *being the teacher* of that event." Professor Gershom said, sitting down, very pleased, a sharp-grin holding, even through the experience of the body rapidly descending because of a foot slipping from the foothold of a stool.

The audience seemed to be pleased as well, at least, they could tell that Gershom was on their side, but not everybody was so sure, that is, throughout the trial, one thing, just kept getting repeated, and every so often, that *thing* that kept getting repeated, would hear itself being spoken by the prosecutor, and then later by Professor Gershom, and each time it was spoken, Raca would pick his head up and look, eyes focusing as if all of the inaction prior had been charging for each subsequent look, *that thing*, was a name, as names were wont to do, in that head of Raca, float around, come up, be said, remind, remind, tell him, talk to him, make him feel, no, it was not things or sentences, but names, for often it was names that were attached to people that made him feel things, and *that name was Stefano.*

"Raca," Professor Gershom now said, sitting uncomfortably, still behind the double desk, "it is finally your turn!"

"My turn?" Raca's head, swiveling in a raw disbelief, he had that same look in eyes that T did, when Marguerite and Hermes had gotten in the back of the car. "What do *you* want from me?"

"Raca," Professor Gershom said now, slightly confused by the outburst, "As we agreed to before you were hired as the investigator, you, in being the investigator, are responsible to come to a clear consensus on the opinion of the audience *present* about whether or not the accused shall be judged."

Raca let the words sail right past his head, they told Raca that he had to reflect the consensus of the present audience, but he had never been on stand before, he had never *had an audience*, there before him, judging him, watching him, he was always the audience, or at least one point he became that way, *alone*, sure he remembers having groups of people standing around him, judging him, it happened basically last week, but never before were they *looking to him*, for his opinion, he didn't know what to do, as far as he could understand it, it was like that episode of *Law & Order*: *Criminal Intent*, that he loved so much, in which two groups, defense contractors, were being investigated by

Detectives Robert Goren and Alex Eames, they had been put on the case when some cyber security employee, Ian Masefield was mysteriously killed, fell to his death, they knew someone had pushed him, but they didn't know who, so they go to dig deeper to find out who might know who did it, and the company, one of the defense contractors, Ascalon Security, Ian worked at didn't know who Ian was, Ian was not listed as an employee, the identification found on the body was fraudulent.

They find out he had been using some lady, Elise Clark's, mailing address as his home address, and when they get there this lady, Elise, tells the detectives that her son Matt is friends with Ian, and Matt let Ian use the address because Ian would travel, but she says she doesn't know where Matt is, so the detectives go to Matt's apartment.

At his apartment they find out he was some sort of hacker, and had been using a fake identity, Ian Masefield, they put it together because there was a trail back to his mom, and whatnot, so when they go back to the mom's place, she's run away from the police, whereas before she was pretending she didn't know anything.

So they start trying to figure out what the *motive* is, and they put together that where Ian, or Matt, had fallen from housed a penthouse apartment of the *other* defense contractor, Sun Tech Industries, and the detectives rightly assume that Matt had also been working there, and they had Matt infiltrate Ascalon as a mole.

When they go back to talk to Ascalon, they recognize Ian Masefield now as being Matt Clark, and profess that they are innocent in response to his death, that they had no idea of the conspiracy.

Anyway, at the scene of the crime, initially, Matt, or Ian, had been found with a black negligee, so that eventually led them to the negligee shop, where they find out that Matt purchased it, present with two bodyguards, and had the negligee then delivered.

At the apartment where it was delivered to, they find that the women there is a krav maga instructor, and that she has a similar tattoo to Matt's, in addition to equipment and gear for hacking the same as Matt.

They bring her back to the precinct to interrogate her, and eventually she reveals that her and Matt both had an agenda to destroy the defense contractors, by leaking their secrets to the public, because the defense contractors were warmongers.

Eventually, the detectives find out that Matt had been corresponding with Wikileaks, and had found secret documents.

And with the height of all the investigating going on, one of the defense contractors, Ascalon, their boss is almost killed by a nearby explosion, which came from an unknown origin.

They assume that this boss was attempted to be killed, for the same reason, that they may have attempted to kill Matt, even though they said they didn't do it, which is that Ascalon had some very sensitive documents, something about a poison pill.

So the two defense contractors start arguing with each other, both through the detectives and on their own time, but nonetheless it is not pulling up any strings, they cannot find the sensitive data, and aren't sure who is really telling the truth, it becomes difficult for them to know what is true.

They do get a match on the tattoo, the one the negligee lady had, and it is connected to the People's Liberation Brigade, which apparently had tried to blow up the bull on Wall Street, so Goren asks to see mugshots of fugitives of the group, and Elise Clark, Matt's mom is one of them.

Eventually, they get Elise Clark in custody, and they question her about the new bomb attack, because it was made with similar techniques as to the bomb during the original attack, against the bull.

She also has the tattoo, and Goren is starting to get upset because he feels like Elise *taught* Matt to be the *revolutionary* he attempted to be before getting killed, and when they go to pursue the negligee lady because evidence links her to the scene of the crime they are unable to find anything incriminating, they start to feel like someone had been hatching a conspiracy that is still playing out.

So Goren goes back to Elise, she is in her detention cell, and he asks her, why she didn't flinch when they first came to her and told her that her son had been killed, and since then she has not been showing the usual signs of grieving, so he pushes her, asking her if she cried after they left and she says to him:

> Elise: "Do you believe in anything beyond that badge? Anything?"

> Goren: "I guess I believe that victims need an advocate."

Elise: "And you put me in a cell? I spent my entire life fighting for the victims of racism, imperialism, of the blind selfishness of capitalism."

Goren: "Was it worth it? Did you bring down the warmongers, the bankers? Did your revolution crush the capitalist system? They're all still here, but your son is gone. Was your revolution worth his life?

From that point the whole pace of the episode changes and Goren and Elise team up to take down the two defense contractors who had been spinning lies and *conspiracies* because of their internal issues that had gotten Matt caught up in all of it.

After that Goren goes to therapy, still thinking about his conversation with Elise, and realizes how much he had stopped thinking about those things, about making a difference, and he begins to feel remorse, this was usually the part of the episode that would go over Raca's head.

He would still be thinking about that one line, again and again, 'victims need an advocate,' he didn't know why he liked it so much, he thought of it fondly as *the motive* for an investigator during a case, a way to rebalance things, because there was so much corruption, so many people creating conspiracies just to keep themselves in the positions of power they had been abusing, mistreating other people, how it would lead to more and more death, and that they'd usually get away with it, push the blame on some revolutionary, he thought these things to himself.

Thinking about the long day he just had, missing these shows he loved so fondly, to witness a trial for most of the day that was either too difficult to understand or too loud to know what was going on, nothing like *Law & Order*, where everything eventually made sense.

He wished he could just watch this trial on television, then he'd be able to tell himself what to do, but he was clueless, and the cluelessness was starting to really get to him, because the audience was sitting there staring at him, as they had been for the last fifteen minutes.

While he sat and thought about all things they had said, and the ways that they would respond to each of his actions, he felt crippled, unable to know which direction to move his mind out of fear that any direction would go against his core principles, how to respect the authority of the court, when the court could be causing a conspiracy, how to give a proper consensus to the opinions of a present group of people who seemed to like to yell or be applauded more than they were interested in the plot of the trial.

inspiration

It had frustrated Raca at several points, and as much as he wanted to lash out at them, *in disdain*, he knew he had to make the right decision, it's just he had no idea what the right decision was, and as he kept thinking the day was starting to end completely, and the sun was now really going down, with its light shifting from across the left side of the audience, where it had been, towards the center aisle, as the sun's light went through the gap between the butterfly-bleachers, where all of the faculty had been sitting this whole time, and cast itself with all its remaining light for that day squarely on stage, there just as the light had apexed the double-desk, sending Professor Gershom into a blindness Raca knows all too well from his own home, the shadow of the stage stretched the long distance of the quadrangle to the alcove appearing on the glass panels by the entrance, allowing the interior of the hallway to be seen, the shadow looked like a U.F.O..

33

Thirteenth Class

...imagine that the boat was launched again and again, and each time it ended when nobody could get the boat to go farther, so, now imagine what it would take for the boat to reach the farthest, this answer could be a composite of many different boat launches, that is, events which within each of them could have occurred, such as certain tasks did better when so and so beliefs and actions happened, whereas others diminished, and each launch different, different folds found ways to become better equipped to sustaining the collective experience, now imagine that it just so happened that one launch had all of these different folds occur at once, that *something* happened, which caused everyone to be able to understand what it is that they needed to do and each were able to without causing disruption to anyone else, that the people of the boat discovered a way to make the boat go on indefinitely, so that it could be said the destination would be arrived to one day if it is ever to be arrived."

"Professor?"

brilliance

"Yes, Mallory?"

"Why would the boat make everyone discover this *best way*, isn't there some limit on the boat that something so utopic isn't possible?"

"Well that is a good suspicion to have, but rather than seeking to conclude *that*, let's assume that something did, and discover what it could *be*, because then with that in hand we can check it against what we know within the composition of the boat to see if it is possible."

CPSIA information can be obtained
at www.ICGtesting.com
Printed in the USA
LVHW040920220423
745007LV00020B/154